ONE HUNDRED APOCALYPSES
AND OTHER APOCALYPSES

ONE HUNDRED
APOCALYPSES
AND OTHER
APOCALYPSES

LUCY CORIN

MᴄSWEENEY'S
SAN FRANCISCO

McSWEENEY'S
SAN FRANCISCO

Cover design by Dan McKinley.
Cover illustrations by Lily Padula.

McSweeney's and colophon are registered trademarks of McSweeney's,
an independent publishing company with wildly fluctuating resources.

McSweeney's is a fiscally sponsored project of SOMArts, a 501(c)(3) nonprofit
organization. This publication is made possible, in part, by generous contributions
from individual donors, foundations, and corporations. We are profoundly
grateful for the support of our readers and supporters around the world.

ISBN: 978-1-940450-02-5

www.mcsweeneys.net

CONTENTS

EYES OF DOGS

A soldier came walking down the road, raw from encounters with the enemy, high on release, walking down the road with no money. He thought he was walking home, but who knows if anyone would be there. The road was lined with trees, and every so often a hovel hunched right there at its edge, droopy and mean, with a dirt yard like a pale sack at its feet. The soldier passed a hovel with a little dog outside, barking on a rope. The dog's dish was just beyond the reach of the rope. He watched the dog run, barking, to reach it, catch itself by the neck at the end of the rope, bounce back yelping, and do this repeatedly, his white ruff following the jerk of his head. The soldier could see that there was nothing in the bowl.

As he walked along, the trees grew broader, filling in the canopy far above. He passed a little girl on the stoop in front of a blackened hovel door, breaking branches into pieces for tinder, wearing a fancy dress gone ragged. He could see, through the tattered ribbons and limp lace bows, that the fabric of the dress had once been rainbow-colored and shiny. The girl's eyes looked very big because of the circles under them, but her skin, smudged as it was with ash, seemed to pulse dimly, just as the shine of the dress did.

At the next hovel, an old woman was stirring a large iron pot set up on coals in the dirt yard. For an instant, the soldier thought that this was his mother. He took his hands from his coat pockets to wave to her, but then he could see that it was not his mother; it was a witch. The resemblance, however, remained, and part of him thought that with all he'd done and seen, he might have made his mother into this. Another part of him still felt the kind of trust and longing you can feel toward a mother, even if she has become a witch after all these years.

The witch called out to him, her face rusty and sweating, beaded with steam, holding a crooked spoon in a hand concealed by her cloak: "Soldier! I see you looking at me with your weird eyes. I can see right through you, and I know what you want."

The soldier said: "What's in the pot?"

He thought, *I bet you think I want to be a better man.*

The witch said: "I know what you want. It's money, and I know where you can get it. There's nothing to it. You just go and get it, and I know where."

She was right. That's what he wanted. He forgot to ask her how it could be that she lived in a hovel and knew where there was money, because there she was, and she was right, he wanted it, so the soldier forgot to ask about that, and about why the witch's hovel sagged to the side and why she wore a witch's rags, and if she had any sons who'd gone off to war, and he forgot about the pot, about what might be stewing and steaming in it. His mind cleared of everything except the idea of money.

"Tie this rope around your waist," said the witch. "Hop down this black hole into this deep hollow tree. You'll be tethered to me. Don't be frightened of what you see. Ha! You've seen worse. You'll see some dogs. Wink at the first dog, blink at the next dog, and for the third, squeeze your eyes shut and wait to see. You will find a little leather purse in the earth down there, and all I ask is: bring it to me. If you don't, I won't pull you up, and *then* you'll have something to be frightened of."

A tinderbox is a little box that sparks to make fire. Like for lighting things. But a purse is what you put your stuff in.

So he wound the rope around his waist and the witch took the loose end. Then he hopped down into the hollow tree and fell deep underground. *Smack!* His feet hit the earth. Everything around him was so dark that he couldn't see. In the dark he thought of the little dog, so stupid for lurching at the end of his leash. He thought of the little girl and recognized the terrible whirl of ideas that had surged across his mind when he saw her: to hack her to pieces, to feed her soup and rock her to sleep, to gobble her up for himself, to dress her properly. He put his hands to the rope around his waist because he was having trouble breathing and felt like it was choking him from the gut up, but soon his eyes adjusted to the light. He could see the twisty shadows of the inner wood of the tree, tunneled with wormholes and mudwasps. It wasn't only his eyes adjusting, though; the light was changing too, and he stepped toward where it pushed at him through the darkness. The light expanded its reach, the space expanded with it, and soon he could see a whole chamber lit with a hundred burning lights.

This reminded him of something, this chamber with passages like fingers out of a glove. Then he remembered: he remembered tearing open a man's belly with his sword in battle, and seeing himself as if within the man's stomach, looking from that chamber down the man's bright bowels, which simultaneously lay beating on the ground before them. And as if summoned by this thought, an enormous blue dog appeared, guarding a golden chest.

The dog had eyes as big as snowglobes, sparkling and swimming with watery light, but the witch was right—the soldier had been through a lot, and very little fazed him. He didn't even need to think about her instructions; it was as if she were there with him, as if he could feel her through the rope. *You need to cut those apron strings and find your way in the world!* That's what people had said to him when they passed him chopping wood for his mother's hovel, that was one thing he'd thought when he enlisted, and that was what was on his mind when he winked at the enormous dog, and the dog lay down and tilted his head to the side and let the snow settle, an Eiffel Tower reflected in one eye, a Golden Pyramid glowing from the depths of the other, and the soldier opened the chest. Out bulged heaps of promissory notes, some slipping to the dirt floor like expiring moths.

This was disappointing. Promissory notes. Would he have to impersonate people in order to collect? Would he spend his life journeying from one debtor to the next along branching paths, shaking people down in a sharkskin suit? It sounded like a crap job, not magic. The soldier looked at the affable dog. "You got me," he said, but he stuffed his pockets anyway. The dog shook his head and the snowglobes snowed and snow settled in heaps on the Statue of Liberty and the Great Wall of China seen from afar. Then the vast lids lowered, and the cavern darkened again.

The soldier felt disoriented, annoyed, betrayed. He felt a rise of panic in the dark. He moved his hand to tug the rope, ready to get up there and give the witch a piece of his mind, but the room began to brighten, this time from the bottom up in sharp fanning shafts as from beneath a rising airplane shade. There before him loomed an even more enormous dog, and bluer, this one grouchily awakening from a nap, yawning, stretching, great shoulderblades shifting like mountains through time, with eyes as big as the capitol dome, magic beaming from beneath the lids as they rose, and the light rose. This dog was so enormous that his head pressed the top of the chamber, which even so must have expanded to accommodate him and his eyes, and the soldier shook minutely in his boots. His mind went blank, and by luck, or the divine, he blinked.

The dog guarded jewels the soldier knew he'd have to hock, but still, they were beautiful to look at, calling to the whole histories of the cultures they came from, dangling golden icons, some inscribed with poetry and the names of families and families of ancestors in uncountable languages and symbologies. Bracelets and brooches, watches and cufflinks, fine times, worth gifted. He dumped the notes and heaped his neck and arms with jewelry. Something about the weight against his naked neck, gravity pulling his limbs to the earth, all these strands from so many lives blotting each other out, wriggling in and out of reach of each other—he started to feel grand, wrapped in everyone's heirlooms. He started to feel that any one of the lives could have been his.

What had he been hoping to find at the end of the road? His mother's arms, his mother dead?

Dog three. Eyes as big as planets, one ringed with rings and one with a great red spot floating gaseously in it. Hallucinatory expansive light, light filled with fire and ghosts, so fragmented and strobing that the soldier squeezed his eyes shut. He shut them not because the witch had told him to; in his terror he had forgotten her, he was on his own, and shutting his eyes was the natural thing to do. With them shut he

LUCY CORIN

could feel them and know that eyes are holes. Beneath his lids the dog fanned like a pack of cards into a pack of dogs, equal and endless. He held his breath, too, until sightless, breathless, the dogs scattered and sent his mind spasming with horrors: a childhood memory (being poked with sticks), a war memory (being poked with swords), an image of that little girl in her blackened rainbow frock and what he was doing that he wanted to do, a blue three-headed dog coming upon his wickedness and tearing him to pieces, stealing the girl to safety, the girl on the back of the blue dog holding the white dog with its ruff in her lap, both of them glancing over their shoulders and receding, watching them recede, spying his limbs strewn in the trees of the forest around him, these ideas and many more, until he was just as frightened of the world behind his eyes as he was of the monster before him, and only because of this equity did he open his eyes to the dog who lay placid as an ocean seen from space, fierce but distant, and entirely content without him.

And this chest held cash, in large bills for saving, in small bills for handy spending. What it suggested was endless possibility anchored in safety, and this time when the sun went behind the eyes of the greatest and most awesome blue dog of all, the soldier nestled in the arms of an economy yet to collapse, dopey in the darkness of the beating chamber. In the womby light he dumped the jewels and lined his boots and cap with bills, stuffed his pockets in a stupor. Then he tugged the cord.

The witch hollered down: "Get that purse!" and he swept his eyes about until he found, in the dog's afterglow, a limp black leather sack with a drawstring mouth, which he snatched as his feet left the ground. Up, up he went, waist-first, empty as a hollow tree. He stood on the road in the forest, eye to eye with the witch, adjusting to the light very nicely. He stood feeling his money, gripping the wrinkled pouch in his fist. "This is what you want?" the soldier said.

"Yes, and give it to me. You have everything," said the witch.

"Do you know my mother?" the soldier asked the witch. He peered at her eyes, which were the eyes of a rat—or who knows, perhaps they were really the eyes of squirming rats that the witch had carved out and taken for her own. Who knew if she'd ever had her own eyes. Who knew what was behind them, if she'd lost them or had them taken from her by her own mother. "I was on my way to find her," said the soldier, holding the purse so she could see it, letting a threatening skepticism control his voice, "when, what do you know, I met *you*."

"Mother smother! Give me that purse. I know some people. How do I know what they do with their loins? I'm just a witch. Give me that purse."

The soldier picked up the rope, which had dropped in a heap from around his waist. He pushed the witch up against the tree so that she blocked the hole in it, and he bound her there.

"Let me go and I'll tell you how to make the purse work," said the witch. "I know you're a bottomless pit and you know too, you fool. You've known it your whole life. Now let me go."

"Tell me first, witch. Tell me or I'll tell everyone who you are, because I know who you are, and I know what you're keeping from me."

"You don't know anything," said the witch. But then she told him. She said: "When you need the purse, the purse will say: 'I am an old purse with a pursed mouth and squeezed-out skin. I am a purse like a pot you put things in. I am the thing from which all things come and go. I am empty and I am full, and that is all you need to know.'"

He feels very full of himself because of the money, so he hacks the witch to pieces with his sword and takes the Tinderbox without really thinking anything of it. Then he goes into town, where he gains respectability, spends lavishly, and eventually has nothing but the Tinderbox left, which he finally notices. He strikes it, to light a candle stub, thinking about a princess that the king and queen have locked away, a bit of light in the darkness of a box. He's heard rumors of her beauty: more glinting in the dark. With the first strike appears the first dog with his great eyes. What does the soldier want? He wants money. Money is fetched. If he strikes twice, there comes the second

LUCY CORIN

dog, with its greater eyes and its more frightening character. Three times and the third dog is raised. Very, very scary, largest-ever eyes. But the first is plenty. The first brings the money, and then, when the soldier asks, the dog fetches the lovely princess from her bed in the night, and in the night the soldier does whatever he wishes with her, which we know, we know what he wishes, and in the morning the girl tells her dreams to her mother, and the queen sends a fleet-footed maid to keep watch. In the night comes the good blue dog with the eyes and the maid runs after him and marks an X on the door to the soldier's apartment, which the dog sees, and marks X's on all the doors in

"That's what the purse will say?"

"Yep. When you need it, that's what the purse will say. You don't need to know anything."

The soldier thought about that. He thought about what he knew about witches from rumors and from experience. "But I still won't know what to do," he said. The more he looked, the more the witch looked both more and less like his mother. He couldn't tell. She kept shifting, being more like his mother in one way but then less in another. He could hardly remember that he had any money at all. He tried to hold on to the thought of having money because of what it meant for his future. But it was slippery.

"You put your mouth to its mouth," said the witch. "You don't call with your voice, but you call with your mind, and your tongue, into the darkness. You close your eyes and feel it there. You will know what to do. You will want what you want, and there it will be."

He gave up making any sense of her, but he could tell she was making fun of him and making him feel lewd. He had been planning to leave her there to encounter some helpful woodland animal or else starve, but instead he took his hunting knife and stabbed her, once, in the stomach, and all the blood and air came rushing out of her until she was one empty black rag sack tied to the tree like something— well, a little like many things but still like nothing he could put a finger on.

He went into town. He went to a bar and challenged a man to darts, and he won beer after beer

16

playing darts. There was a girl he recognized from high school who did not recognize him back. They went to her place. She'd grown much older than he had. He tried to see the girl she might have become within the girl she was, but all he could see was her. They ate cheese and crackers from her cabinets and she was happy to do just about any sexual thing you can think of with him, which they did for several hours, although her skin was bad and she was drunk and so emotionally confusing he stopped paying attention. In the morning, light slid in enough to show all the dirt. Her place smelled like the inside of a body.

"Aren't you going to take me to breakfast, even?" she asked. First he said: "Sure, I'll take you anywhere you want. I'll take you places you've never been," but then he reached into his pockets, just to lay his fingers on his cash, and there was nothing in there but a handful of ash, and same in his boots, and same in his hat. So he went into the hallway, his heart frantic, and stared at the purse, willing it to speak, but it said nothing. So he ripped at the mouth of the purse until it opened. He put his mouth to its mouth, though it disgusted him more than anything, more than the girl with her pustuled skin, or the witch before her, or any moment in any war he'd known or heard of, or anything his mother could ever have done or said, no matter what she ever really did or said, or any thought he'd ever had that he'd ever tried not to think. There has never been a thing so awful as being mouth to mouth and there's nothing there. Oh god,

town, but is foiled the next night by a trail of flour from a bag with a hole in it stashed under the girl's skirt, and so the soldier is caught and set to be hanged for his crimes. There on the scaffold, with the rope around his neck, he asks for his Tinderbox so he might have one last smoke, and it is brought to him. So he strikes once, and twice, and three times, and there come the dogs who tear the king and queen to pieces and also much of the town and its people. Those who remain make the soldier king, and he marries the princess, who is said to enjoy being queen very much—all plausible enough, except perhaps for the part about flour.

and what about the dogs, what about the dogs, saying nothing, so blue and enormous, with their eyes, with everything in the world, fierce and dopey and incomprehensible. Never coming to our rescue even when we don't deserve it.

MADMEN

The day I got my period, my mother and father took me to pick my madman. The whole time, my dad kept his hands in his pockets and my mom acted like it was her show. I hadn't let her in on how scared I was that I might be a freak born with endometrial tissue of steel. Apparently it didn't cross her mind that I might be worried, watching all my friends go through it and what was up with my body. I stopped digging, looked in my pants, and told her what was going on in there, and what she said was, "All right, but hurry and get back out here."

It was getting toward lunch and we were digging a drainage ditch from the shed down to the woods. With my lateness, our preparations had become elaborate. We thought of everything, and my madman was going to really like his situation, I felt sure. We had a couple chickens he could take care of or else eat. Some of the almond trees still dropped nuts, and who doesn't like nuts? We had a circle of rocks for a fire pit with a view of the creek and an iron pot handed down from my grandmother, the one that her madman used and her father's madman used before that. In the shed I'd hung the curtains from my room before I was old enough to make my own decisions. They had a tassel fringe that I thought looked like paper-chain dolls with their hands merged together.

So I ran inside and did my best to remember what she'd told me about tampons when I was like ten, and then I ran back out and we finished the ditch even though I felt heavy and gross. In the shed we freshened up the straw, and then I went back inside *again* to shower while my mom called my dad at work so he could meet us. A lot of people would consider my mother grim, but I could hear her on the phone, at least until I turned on the water, and she sounded excited about taking me for my big day.

In the shower, I thought about my madman. It was getting hotter, so there were going to be a lot to choose from. Over the weekend, at my friend Carrie's birthday, we'd told our fortunes with a question-naire we found online. Her madman wouldn't come out but we'd heard the basics about him. For what kind of house I wanted I put *Treehouse*, *Houseboat*, *Malibu Mansion*, and for my risk choice, *Outhouse*. If you don't put a risk, it undermines the integrity. For what kind of job I put *Parachuter*, *Famous Scientist*, *Hang-Gliding Instructor*, and *World Peace*—which isn't a job, but it's the thought that counts. For who I was going to marry I put *Anthony*, *No One*, *A Lesbian*, and *Yo' Mama*. For pet I put *Yo' Mama*, *Giraffe*, *Ant Farm*, and *Crabs*. I was completely not being serious by the time I got to car because I know I'm never getting a car so I just put *Anything*, *Flying Saucer*, *Argh!!!*, and *Who cares my parents are never getting me a car* (though the window only had room for twenty characters, so it ended up *Who cares my parent*). But the point is I got serious with the madman question. Even kids who seem like they don't care about their madman are faking it. They care.

"How did you know which madman was yours?" I asked Carrie later, in private. She said she looked each of them in the eyes, even just for a fraction of a second with the fast ones, but then with her madman she got them to take her into his cell—he was in the far back corner and she'd almost thought the cell was empty. He was pale and "Seriously," she said, "I know it's hard to believe, but he *blended in*." I wondered if he was an albino madman, which suddenly seemed exotic and perfect.

"Is that how you knew?" I asked.

"No," she said. All the other girls were asleep. It was dark and we were near the window, face to face with our legs over opposite arms of a giant overstuffed chair, with the black sky surrounding us and everyone's sleeping bags covering the living room floor. It was like we were in a rowboat, bobbing in a sea made of our sleeping friends. "I went in and he wouldn't look at me. I put my hand on his chin like this, you know, like when an older man wants to kiss you in the movies." She shrugged. It seemed like our boat rocked. "I know that sounds creepy, but it's not. I just felt older than him, and he kept turning his chin and not looking at me."

"Will he look at you now?" I asked.

"That's not the point," she said. "Plus none of your beeswax." She said she picked that phrase up from her madman.

I wanted one like my uncle had, who was an accomplished musician. Special. Or one time I was downtown, some girl was totally engrossed in window shopping, and her madman was sniffing around the sidewalk, lifting pebbles with his toes, humming very low, very soothing. I pretended like I was window shopping too, to get closer, and when I caught the tune, it didn't even seem to be coming from him. More like it was surrounding him, moving through him, something like religion, or wisdom. Some people would be surprised how important wisdom is to me. I try to remember what he hummed, but I was young and I can't remember. I mean, I know I'm still young. But your brain changes.

Deep in the night I woke up and it was just me in the giant chair. Across the room, across the ocean of sleeping girls like waves, I saw Carrie and her madman in the doorway that went into the kitchen. They were silhouetted, standing forehead to forehead, passing a sandwich back and forth. Then the madman reached over and tugged on a handful of her hair. Like ringing a bell, but soft. Then Carrie reached over for a handful of his hair and tugged back.

Of course I don't remember my online fortune, that's never the part that sticks, and no one believes it anyhow. It's more about answering the questions plus what you're willing to tell people.

The shower went predictably. After my shower, I went right for the skirt and blouse I thought were a perfect balance of mature and still had hints of my personality. But once I put it on it was more like a combination of pretentious and someone who was not trustworthy. I started from scratch. I picked my underwear—serious underwear, but new. Car-crash undies. Then I picked footwear: dressy boots with square heels. Once you know the shoes, that narrows your options. Soon my mom was screaming for me. "It's not a beauty pageant!" I don't know why she has to scream, the house is not that big. I guess it doesn't matter what I was wearing. But it does to me.

All the way in the car I wished I had skipped the tampon and went with a pad. It must have been in crooked, but at the time I thought this must be what it's like. My mom, who is a bad driver and also incredibly opinionated about driving, was on her cell phone talking a hundred percent understandingly about someone in the hospital after an incident in the home, and then suddenly on another call, a hundred percent enthusiastically about someone's idea for self-catering a wedding in a schoolhouse on a cliff. She's not faking, either. Endless empathy, one person after another, all day long, like a buffet. I just wanted my madman.

Meanwhile I watched the world go by out the side window, comparing regular view versus including the mirror. I kept wondering if the world was going to look different after I had a madman, so I wanted to get a good "before" shot of it. To sum up, the world was: green, green, green, house, street, green, gas station, green, green, strip mall, green with brown, then hillier and hillier. Then, exactly as my mother was saying "schoolhouse" again, we went by this little white schoolhouse I'd never noticed before. It was as if her saying the word "schoolhouse" made it appear—I was so surprised I tried to point it out to her, but she shook her head not to interrupt, and by then she'd missed it. Or maybe it was a church.

It had its own velvet hill. It had a weathervane. A deer ate puffs of grass the mower had missed by its front steps. A motorcycle was parked nearby, tilted on its kickstand. It looked like it was thinking. The weathervane was spinning, so I couldn't tell what it was, a horse, a whale... It didn't seem windy out, but it's hard to tell. Being in the car was like another planet.

I know it sounds stupid, but this was a big day for me, and everything felt like it might be important at any second.

After a few more hills, the facility rose up in the middle of nowhere. Ours was a nice facility, known to be professional and well equipped, but in some counties it could be hard, even dangerous to go, and some kids brought their whole extended families for protection. In those counties some kids ended up with a madman who died almost immediately. That's meaningful to go through, but it's better if you have time for a broader perspective. The building looked like a normal white country inn, but closer up you could see it went on and on down the hill. We pulled into the parking lot and my mother stopped the car by as usual bumping into the curb. Maybe three other cars were spaced out in the lot, and two beat-up vans. My mother was still working on her phone call, though she did make some eye contact with me, meaning "just a minute." The person would never know, from her nodding and assenting noises, that she was in any way ready to get off the phone, which she never really is. It's the empathy. She loves to empathize. Sometimes I feel bad because maybe I don't. She dove her hand into her purse, which sat open on the seat beside her, the most crammed thing in history, and dragged out a length of crinkled toilet paper because she doesn't believe in kleenex. My mother was admirable—for example, trying to teach me to be the last person on earth resisting the corporate identity takeover of personhood. It made me so angry at myself when I just wanted her to go away, which is not the same as wanting her to die, although she will never understand the difference. She blew her nose using one hand and pushed the toilet paper back into the purse.

Oh my god we were still in the parking lot. When I tapped her on the shoulder she looked about to smack me so I just sat there, probably the fastest route to her hanging up anyway. But I was resenting getting into a bad mood. My phone, for instance, was on vibrate for privacy on the occasion, and the last thing I needed was to be in a bad mood making a decision like this. She kept being herself on the phone. I got angrier and angrier. Then luckily my dad pulled into the spot next to us. I jumped out of the car to meet him, and he's such a huge dork, he never knows what to do, but then sometimes he does exactly the right thing, and this time he got out of his truck with a shopping bag with a bow stuck on it because he can't wrap boxes, although it's funny when he tries.

I hugged him and took the bag. "What have we *here!*" I said, and dug in. It was a harness for my madman, the best kind, made of real leather with quality hand-stitching and brass appointments. My mother came around the car, stuffing her phone into her purse, saying, "Poor Irene!" She was about to launch into recounting everything from the phone, and it's true that Irene's life is pretty shocking and worth hearing about, but all I thought was, *Isn't there a time and a place?* I handed her the gift bag for her to put in the car and catch the hint. She put her hand on my head and I could see her deciding whether to say something or not. For good reason she didn't know if expressing her opinion was the best idea when it came to getting me to feel what she wanted. Finally she just plunked my gift into the back of Dad's truck and said, "Here we go."

We stepped up to the giant double doors, the kind with wire netting between the panes, and I buzzed the buzzer. A plaque on a rock by the stoop read AN ATTACHMENT TO ONESELF IS THE FIRST SIGN OF MADNESS. It was riveted under an engraving of a Ship of Fools, a little hard to see but you could tell it was a really good artist. A woman's face appeared in the window, filling it with puffy red hair, and I thought I was making it up, but she had the kind of eyes a cat has—golden with black diamond-shaped slits instead of pupils. I grabbed my dad's hand in the midst of a flashback to *The Wizard of Oz* where I'm Dorothy and Oz is the door-man but you don't know it yet. My dad held my ID up to the window. She let us in. She wrote some stuff down from my ID and then gave it back to me. She was obviously really nice, but I couldn't look at her. She sat us in the waiting room with another family and left through another set of double doors. This family was one with a boy who must have been turning thirteen, which is when they get theirs. It's really unfair. They should have to go when they start splooging in the night or whatever. God, boys are known for being immature in general, but this one seemed especially short, making me feel extra freakish, that everyone has their madman already and here I am with this kid with a *cowlick*. But I went right over and plunked down next to him and asked, "What is up with her eyes?"

He said, "It's just a disease. My dad's a doctor. Dad, what's it again?"

His dad was reading a magazine about cars. "Coloboma of the iris," he said. His mother was sitting so close to his dad that their thighs touched all the way to the knee. Her magazine was called *Pet City*.

I whispered to the boy, "God, if I wasn't already crazy and she was my nurse, I think I'd go crazy." I could tell he thought I was making light of the situation, but I wasn't.

"She's nice," he said.

I said, "I know."

I was nervous, and I was going to remember this for the rest of my life. There was a nurses' station, but when I went over no one was at it. I slid the window open and put my head through. All I saw was extra pamphlets and forms piled around a computer, but I still felt sneaky so I stopped looking. Soon enough the red-haired cat-eyed nurse returned and the boy went through the double doors into the back with his mom, dad, and cowlick. My mom took another call and the room echoed with her voice. My dad walked around inspecting things—looking into the nurses' station to see what I'd been looking at, squinting at a poster, pressing a thumb into the cushion on the chair like meat to test it for doneness, picking a stray bit of paint from the glass of the window that looked onto the parking lot. He was trying to find something to comment on. He picked up a pamphlet from a rack and started to say something but swallowed it and pretended to be chuckling to himself. There's no such thing as chuckling to yourself. You do it so someone will notice, even if you're by yourself and the person is imaginary. My parents are such a classic couple. They'll either get divorced or he'll get smaller and smaller and she'll get bigger and bigger until they die. Then the red-haired cat-eyed nurse came through the double doors with a smile like homemade pie and said, "Ready, sweetheart?"

"Remember," my mother said, "you, too, could grow up to be a madman."

Shut up, Mom. No one cares about this more than I do.

The gallery was white and clean, and everything—the bars on the cells, the bars on the beds in the cells, even the chamber pots—seemed thicker because of layers of white paint, the sheets fragile by comparison. How could Carrie have looked each one in the eyes? The hall was narrow and endless, like a mirror facing a mirror. You could never look into all those eyes. The space swam with light and occasional arms of madmen waved through the bars. The ceiling was so white it disappeared. Cells lined one side, and the other side was a vast blank wall to walk along. This meant that you could only look into one cell at a time, but if you stayed near the wall you could keep out of reach. I could hear, dimly, that there was an army, like millions of them, beyond the walls. It was the sound of madmen who were not ready. My mother gripped my elbow and adjusted the strap of her purse.

I know from case studies in our Health and Human Development book that when a madman is reeling with madness it's like his skin is ripped off, his consciousness is that naked. Just stepping from the entry-way into view of the first cell I felt something—a wave—like there was empty space left where all these people had been so naked and now I was standing in it. The madman in there wasn't even looking at me and I felt it. In fact, he was facing the back wall. He was bare and yellowish, with the knobs of his spine poking out and a cloth tied around his waist. He might have been peeing, my first potential madman. But he might have just been standing there, looking at the wall. I was just standing there, looking at the bars, with my mom latched to my elbow. Hands deep in his pockets, my father approached the laminated information card at the first madman's cell and read it for our information in a low voice while I took in this prospect with my eyes.

He was a Melancholic madman. He glanced at us absently and then took a seat in a back corner of the cell on a three-legged stool, resting his chin on his fist.

"Appearance: gloomy brow, shrunken head, lethargic, passive," my father read. "Medical history: mad with grief after violating his word to his wife; shunned men and fled to the forest."

"I don't know, what do you think?" said my mother.

"I don't know," I said. I didn't know what to do—imagine my life as his, or imagine him in my life, or what. At some point the nurse had left, and I felt very alone.

29

"Let's look at another," my mother said, and I knew that meant he would be fine for another girl, but not for us. I'd settled on picturing him on his stool by the window in our shed with his gloomy brow, in his thinking position. Where was I in this picture? Was I stirring his pot? Was I pulling up a stool of my own to sit beside him? Was he starting to cry? We stepped to the next cell.

This madman paced and a broken chain from one arm dragged on the ground. He had heaping wads of wiry hair.

"Appearance," read my father. My mother craned her neck over his shoulder at the card, to keep an eye on if he'd miss something. "A bold, threatening mien, a hurried step, splayed gait, restless hands, violent breathing." In the madman's hair I could see a bird's nest and part of a blue eggshell. His eyes moved mechanically in his head, like they had little rollers behind them, but I could hear him making low animal noises of being alive. His sandals slapped the floor as he paced, making angrier slaps than I thought sandals could even make. Heat came off him like from a toaster. Then he whirled to face me, looked right at me, and said, "I heard that, pussy," and before I could even register this, my mother had yanked me to the next cell.

"Perverts are still madmen, but don't pick a pervert just to pick a pervert," she said.

The madman with the nest called, "I can fucking hear you!"

But it was interesting—as soon as we were no longer in front of his cell, it was as if we'd changed the channel. I could hear the dull white noise of whatever world tumbled down the hill behind the gallery, but it must have been something with the acoustics because I could no longer hear the madman at all—not his breathing or his sandals or his chain or anything he might have yelled—not once I was looking into the next cell. They'd really made things orderly. Or my brain had done it. But either way. I saw so many madmen that day: the whole world was made of one madman, and then it was made of the next.

The next was a Decadent Hedon, hunched under a burlap robe, but I could tell by the way the folds fell that he was leaning on a crook: "Appearance" (my mother reading this time), "slothful, bloated, swarthy, indolent, irresolute, fair hair, eburnated protrusions, overall sour." His sleeve slipped and showed a hand, but immediately he shifted just enough for the cloth to cover it again. He had long nails. "Medical history: succumbed to the folly of the idle rich. Discovered inebriated at a marina." My mother read it like a schoolchild, or a schoolteacher, that voice. Even though the Decadent Hedon ignored us, I felt embarrassed with my parents reading as if he wasn't there. I kept trying to look at him in a way that would let him know. Then I thought, *What, should we not read the information?* That's when I said, "Hello, I'm Alice." I didn't expect any one thing or another. On impulse I guess I thought he might appreciate it.

"Fantastico," said the madman, rolling his eyes either at me or because that's what madmen do. The tone, though, was pretty obviously "You know what I mean, you pawn/idiot/cracker/et cetera."

I thought of our shed and the curtains from my bedroom. I knew a madman like that wouldn't like me. He didn't say anything else, in fact he went right back to not acknowledging that we were there, just gazed, lazy-eyed, as if over a vast tabletop, through the wall behind me, through the waiting area beyond it, and out over the hills and valleys of whatever the hell he thought of the world.

I felt ashamed that I wanted so badly for my madman to like me. Like this was all about me. Which it was. I was the one coming of age.

I don't know how I got us to the next one. Oh, yes I do: my mother said, "Honey, have a look at this."

This one was Contemporary Bipolar. Like two for one. He was low, now, "sickly, peevish, having suffered a recent rejection of a manuscript he'd sent to an important publisher." I'm paraphrasing what my father read. They'd found him holding court in a city park, where everyone called him Professor, wearing round glasses with no glass in them. He had this enthusiastic teenage boy who'd follow him around with an apple crate to stand on. Mom observed that you could tell different doctors wrote up the information cards. She said this one had been in a creative mood. The conclusion of the medical history was that this madman was the son of a lowly cleaning lady and had never been to college. It marveled that he could be so erudite in his philosophies, though the doctor confessed he had not heard of many of the figures the madman liked to quote. He was not sure if this was a measure of his own ignorance, as he had only taken introductory courses in the classics, and although he had done very well in them, it had been a long time ago. My father attempted a knowing glance at my mother, which she rejected. He whispered to me, "Next thing you know, that doctor's gonna be eating a madeline."

I said, "What are you talking about?" and then I felt bad.

Next there was a woman madman: "with monstrous breasts, contorted, black"—actually, the madmen were a variety of races and racial mixtures, but this card pointed out *black* for some reason—"eyes bulging, head and arms thrown back, clothes discarded on the floor" (all noted on the card, as well as true to my observation), "with a madman's staff, clenching hands, found biting her own arm, broken out of chains, bold, brazen, brainless"; then a Cretin, with his wiener in a bottle, peeing, then holding the bottle up and looking in it with a monocle ("He's imitating his physician," my father interpreted, "monkey see monkey do"; to which my mother flashed him a look about insensitively using a monkey analogy and he said, "I'm just explaining!"); a Cuckold wearing a Cuckold's horns, I don't know what they were made out of but they looked real; a Schizo-affective who on his card it said "mute" and explained that like so many, he'd latched on, in an early delusion, to where the Bible says, "if thy eye offend thee, pluck it out," a sentence which, gathering from my education, has resulted in madmen missing just about every body part you can think of, but this madman had cut his tongue out, and then, to cauterize it, stuffed a flaming torch down his throat. Mom: "*Cauterize* means seal up"; me: "I know," but I didn't. Then a Possessed guy with landscape tattoos. Then a short guy evolving into a divine being, officially Monomaniac, with sticks stuck into his hair like a crown, trying to look down on us. Next a Wildman dragging a club, with a face like a "panther or a goat," this heavy lumpy body, like he'd broken everything and healed back wrong; then a Phlegmatic, "sad, recumbent, forgetful, pale, eating the bread of the workers of iniquity... protruding eyes, weak chin, terror"; and next a rich girl whose secret lover had joined the army and died. Then Frenetic. Fevered delirium, "raving but seated, ready to be purged." Drawings on one wall of his cell showed a warden after a patient with a billy club and a doctor after a patient with a needle, and on another wall a drawing of being looked at by two tall people with a short one. The one with most detail I recognized from our textbook: an operation to remove the Stone of Folly. The doctor had given the madman the stone just cut from his head, and the madman held it in the air like a jewel. The drawing showed it glinting with light. The drawings were good, considering they'd been done with a stick and fingers and who knows what for paint.

I got dizzy on and off through the madmen, partly because all the iron in my body was rushing out between my legs but also because of the madness. After the Recumbent Frenetic was a pair of cells each containing a Fool, dancing, a man fool and next door to him a woman fool: one with a feather headdress, one with bells around the wrists and ankles. Lighthearted types, goiter on the neck of one, one with a pink balloon on a branch of a bifurcated stick, counterparts dancing like mirror images—how could they know through the wall? It didn't make sense to look at them individually, but I couldn't see both cells at once. The gallery was too narrow, I couldn't back up enough, so I looked from one to the other trying, but it made me feel seasick. I felt at odds with myself, that phrase came to me. Like I was related to whatever invisible puppet master was making them dance together when they couldn't even see each other. I think I spent less time with them than anyone, but the effect went straight to my body.

Plus there was the madman in the cell right after them.

This one had an information card that folded out like an accordion. "At sixteen," my father read, "she became insane over the favor her older sister received from a young man, her husband, so that she was institutionalized."

"Whose husband?" my mother asked. "Who lets these people write?" My mother had continued her commentary all through the gallery; I'd just tuned most of it out. But the point here is this madman's huge long history:

"Periodic manias, daily three to six in the afternoon. Much of the day she behaved normally, but from noon until three sank into the deepest melancholy. Following that she would become lively, and at exactly three in the afternoon she would get a fit of rage and smash everything, attack her attendants and drink enormous amounts of ice water. At six she would become calm again. Taken in by a family when she was seventeen, who, within a year, interrupted three suicide attempts with a silk cord." My mother, again concerned with grammar, wondered how the family might have used a silk cord thusly. But the story went that the girl was finally found so dead she was almost black (I hadn't known this about death), but they revived her, and while they were deciding what to do with her next, she disappeared. Turned out she wanted to be a dancer, which I used to want to be myself, and started working at strip clubs by night and taking dance classes by day and through her stripper and dance friends met up with a troupe of trapeze artists who went across the country and Europe, meeting up with circuses and innovative performing groups, putting on intense acts that, for certain invite-only audiences, were rumored to contain explicit sex with emotional and intellectual depth. A distinguished artist within this community, her prison record called it Live Queer Porn. "And yet," said the account, "such transgressions often bear the germs of healing in them."

Then something happened. The account said: "suddenly." Suddenly she quit the troupe, burned her costumes, wrapped herself in rags, took up a staff of madness decorated with shells, strung a crucifix around her neck, and joined a group of pilgrims on their way to Rome. They were a whole group of people who felt bad about themselves so they went to Rome, but when they got there, the girl threw her rags into the Tiber and wouldn't go into the cathedral. She slept in the Colosseum for months. Then something else happened which I forgot, and probably they skipped some stuff, and she ended up at a mission taking care of orphans even though she refused to wear the crucifix or explain what she was praying, which she was allowed to do because she'd impressed all the religious people, one of whom eventually fell in love with her, ruining his career, but she wasn't interested in him like that, and this whole episode seemed to wear her out, so she kissed her orphans goodbye one by one and then left on a boat in the night, which wrecked in a storm near Messina, where she washed up and was taken in by a group of shepherds—her feet were all cut up—until she could walk, by which time the local doctor had fallen for her and kept inventing medical problems so she'd stay. But once she figured that out, he just left everything and went with her through a junglelike landscape until one night they were accosted. She cut the thumbs off the assailant and escaped, but the doctor was killed. There was definitely some more religion, stone temples, shamans and stuff, Amazons, and a battle she helped win with poison she discovered in local sap, but she started drinking heavily and rather than admit her addiction to her tribe, she slunk into the jungle where she lived on fruit and roots—that'll dry you out—and then something else and she ended up here, in godforsaken nowhere California, after an episode not far from my school actually, where she had been "excessively frightened by soldiers" is how the write-up put it, please note the air quotes which are so annoying but I'm serious because I believe I've heard about those assholes.

You'd think she'd look like a model but she didn't—she was plump and ordinary, with small features and a round, almost silly nose, her eyes and skin sort of pulled out of place a fraction. And you'd think to have done all those things she'd be old, but she seemed more like she could be my sister just done with college with a place of her own. My mother said the doctors were obviously believing her delusions, and she was going to ask the cat-eyed nurse if this was some kind of test, but god, Mom, can't you just have an interesting life? Or is it like everyone really does end up with one of four kinds of cars and one of four kinds of house and one of four kids you met in junior high?

Obviously, this is the madman I wanted. Obviously, my mother said no.

I'm paraphrasing.

This is my day, I told her. This is the one day that of all days is my day and it's not up to you. This decision is going to make me who I am. The woman madman, round and rosy, watched me yelling at my mother with a small smile on her face, looking somewhere between our yelling heads. I don't know what my father was doing. I was so angry. Sometimes when I get really angry, I get really articulate. I said exactly what I was thinking, exactly the way I would want to have said it. But it doesn't matter if you're right, if you made your case, and it doesn't matter if god, somewhere, is on your side. Whatever happens, happens anyway. My mother said obviously they were trying to pawn this madman off, otherwise why would her case history be ten times longer than anyone else's? I said I didn't care if it was all lies, I loved her. I said I felt inspired and connected, at which point the rosy woman looked at me like I was crazy, and her eyes went right into mine, and I could feel my feelings flaring behind my eyes, just as her feelings were flaring behind hers, lighting them up, so I knew we were both lit up, so I knew at least in that way I was right.

Well, that's what it was like at the time. I don't know. You get caught up in a moment.

It seemed real.

I said okay, whatever, I'll take the dancing Fools. My mother was so mad her lips had disappeared. I still don't know where my father was. And I don't know what the madmen were thinking of all this yelling. They've seen it all, anyway. I could sort of hear some laughing, but who knows at what, and again the acoustics. Me and my mom having out this scene, and in front of a completely undeterminable audience, if that's even a word. When we were finally silent and I finally looked at her again, she was building up to say something and then swallowing it and then building up again. When she finally said it, she said it like it was the worst, meanest thing she could possibly say.

"*You are on your own*" is what she finally pronounced, and because she said it to be the meanest possible thing to say, it was.

As we learned in class, when madness comes, it comes up the spine and radiates. Madman after madman has described it this way through history, often saying they were touched by god. Of course that's not what I felt from my mother—boy, she would love that—but my point is it was very physical receiving her words, like being iced over and then cracked. I thought of madness while I felt it. Then she stormed away down the hall, which would have had more of the abrupt effect she was after except the hall was so long she kind of dissipated down it. Plus, after a couple minutes of me watching her recede, still gasping from how mean she was, my father appeared from behind me and followed after her like a can trailing a car when you just got married. *Boom* went the double doors, way far away, or *whoosh* or something. I don't even remember, but it seemed to let noise out from behind the scenes, and even though I know the doors went to the waiting room, what came out

LUCY CORIN

was what you'd expect from those vast back rooms that spilled down the hill behind the asylum: babbling, screaming.

The whole idea is you take in a madman and that teaches you about Facing the Incomprehensible and Understanding Across Difference, and soon we are one big family. Without looking at her again, I left my place in front of the cell of the rosy woman I'd wanted and stared into the cell of the Imbecile who was next. What had he been doing through all that with his lumpy head and beaky honker? It felt like a betrayal to even stand there, to even try to imagine who he was, so I turned around.

Turning around meant I faced a white wall. It occurred to me that I was seeing exactly what all the madmen see, but without the bars. What's that developmental stage called when you can finally do abstract thinking? Algebra? Just kidding.

I didn't want to look at any more madmen. I sat down on the floor. I kept looking at the wall. It was so white.

Then the double doors swung open and smacked the walls with an echoing bang, and then *thump thump* came the cat-eyed nurse with her outward-reaching hair and rubber shoes making squeaks every few steps. Hands came waving through bars as she stomped toward me, though as she neared I could see she wasn't angry at all, or stomping, it was just the sound of moving down that unpredictable gallery. Some hands she slapped five or did twinkle fingers with, and quips went back and forth that I couldn't hear. She got to me and stood with her hands on her hips and gazed down at me mock-somethingly, which got me sheepish, as I'm sure she intended.

"You seriously want the Dancing Fools," she said.

"Yes."

"*That* I would not have predicted." She walked a little circle around me, shaking her red mane, and I pretended I wasn't freaked out to look at her, and after a few seconds of pretending, it was true. *I'm not freaked out by a cat*, I thought, *and I'm not freaked out by a nurse. So where's the problem?* That's where I was, emotionally. "Do you *dare* me to give you the Fools?" she asked.

"No, I don't *dare* you, it's just what I pick."

She stopped and crouched next to me. She was wearing orange tights with her white uniform and I hadn't even noticed it before. Now that the rest of her was normal, the tights could look crazy.

"Look, miss. I get 'rude' all day from people like *them*," she said. "Do you think I need 'rude' from *you?*" I could feel her looking at me, but no matter how much of a problem I didn't have with her I could not look directly into those fucked-up golden orbs of doom, and just like that, her life stretched before me: one endless gallery of madmen seen as if through a keyhole because of my catty eyes. I had one cat-eyed kid left from a litter lost tragically, and a husband always out on the prowl.

I'm kidding.

What happened is off I hopped from my high horse because she was nice, she was right about me, and I didn't need to understand her back.

She pulled a small spiral notebook from the front pocket of her skirt. There was a list of names in handwriting that looked like calligraphy: Bobo, Kai, Armand, Kelly. "These are all fine choices, and they all like you fine," she said. I hadn't seen any of them yet. They were farther down the gallery. Maybe there was an information card on me. The kingdom of the mad is inexhaustible, as they say. I knew a kid once whose parents were against the madman system, and he got out of it by spending summers building houses for the poor and taking a test on human rights history. I was glad my parents weren't around to interfere, but I still thought of that kid's parents, parents like one thing, like conjoined twins, but reverse: of two bodies and one mind.

Then suddenly I thought I felt blood spilling out of me and I stood up in a panic, like a rabbit on the highway, no idea which way to go. It was awful. Along with my boots, I was wearing brown pants that were plain but just cut really nice for my body, but I hadn't been thinking, when I put them on, about my period and all that could happen. I had no idea what would happen with this color pants if I leaked. The madman in the cell behind me, the imbecile with the head and the beak, who at some point had snuggled up with his sheet on his cot and was possibly sleeping, sat up with a jerk and said, in a voice that sounded not like an imbecile talking back to a dream, not like an imbecile at all: "No, please, not me. I'll do anything. I've got a bad feeling about you."

"You want to meet them?" said the nurse, still holding out her spiral notebook.

"I need to go to deal with my period," I said. "I'll take Armand."

Honestly, I know that in some cultures girls are supposed to feel shame over their period, and it's not like I feel anyone should be ashamed of what they are, but if you're like, "Oh, the flow of my blood, the essence of my womanhood," well, that is just stupid and disgusting. There I am with my responsible-looking pants on the handbag hook in the stall, standing in my socks and, oh yeah, my naked ass, at the counter wiping blood off my crash-appropriate underwear with a paper towel. What, then, is least disgusting: put your underwear back on all damp and horrific, put your underwear on inside out so the damp part rubs up on your favorite and nicest pants, put them back on and stuff them with toilet paper that might fall down your leg at any second, don't put them back on and hope you don't leak again until you can get more underwear and perhaps a *panty liner* which why didn't your mother fucking suggest this ever, and why have you never seen any panty liners in the house? Perhaps it is your mother that is disgusting. And even then where do you put your underwear, in your pocket or what? Because you left your bag in the car because you wanted your hands free for picking out your madman. Not to mention I thought this place was so well equipped, and hasn't anyone ever noticed that girls who are on the *first* day of their *first* period and don't know what they're doing come here all the time? So where's looking that in the eyes and understanding it? So also, as Carrie would say, none of your beeswax about what is least disgusting in my worldview.

Outside the bathroom the nurse was waiting for me, leaning on the wall like she's from the '50s.

"You okay?"

"Yes," I said.

"Armand, still? You sure?"

"Yes."

She smiled, then, a 100 percent genuine smile which there's no faking. I know, because I have watched myself in the mirror and tried.

So his name was Armand, and in that way my madman transformed from a madman to the name of a man, which is only a little different but counts at least some. The nurse pushed back through one set of double doors to go get him ready, and I pushed through another, into the waiting room with a pile of forms and my vacant parents who were staring at posters on opposite ends as if they were looking out portholes in a ship. Where their heads weren't blocking, I could see that one poster was a phrenology diagram, and the other was a color-coded brain scan. Were they even looking at what they were looking at? Twinges in my belly were either anxiety or cramps or both. I didn't know anyone who'd just picked a name from a list on advice from a psychiatric/psychotic-looking nurse. But I know you can never pick exactly right. There'd be a whole other batch any other day. One day you could walk in and it's your old friend Bitsy from second grade wearing a rag and picking her butt and looking at you and the space next to you like it's the same thing. Which maybe it is. I didn't throw a dart, but the way I chose my madman had very little magic in it, and what should I learn from that?

Well, it had a little magic, like a pebble in a setting forged for a diamond. *Oh, Armand*, I thought. *My own little pebble.* The phrase came back to me: *coloboma of the iris*, and it sounded like a lullaby.

Meanwhile, I handed some forms to my dad and we sat as if peacefully doing paperwork while all the weight in the room slid toward the black hole created by my mother as she ignored us both. I'd missed something, something between them, and probably something with the nurse, as well. I asked my dad, I guess to break the ice, "Why do so many of them have sticks?" because all I knew about my madman was, according to the nurse, he was not going to leave his behind and I should be okay with that. And his cloak.

"Staffs," my father said, considering. "Shepherds used to carry crooks. Madmen have traditions."

"What they have," my mother said, still focused on the phrenology poster, "is a brain disorder."

I pictured sheep like marbles, always wandering off, pictured a madman named Armand on a grassy hill, his marbles rolling away, trying to pull them back with his crook, useless. How far he must have traveled, hiking back roads and mountain trails, fording creeks with it, balancing with three legs. I pictured that. How he might have speared a fish with it, or clubbed a rabbit over the head to eat, or slayed an enemy in the night. Or used it for a wand, to turn seawater potable, to ward off evil, to punish his tormentors. Or the stick was bifurcated. It split. In order to represent his brain.

"Okay, geniuses, perhaps it's not a brain disorder," my mother said, as if anyone had said anything. "He's been emasculated by his madness. In fact, it's a dick. Let him have it. It makes him feel better." Unsurprisingly, this seemed to hurt my father's feelings. It also appeared that while she was not yet talking to me, she wanted me to know she was there, so that was a good sign.

The nurse materialized in the nurses' station and I met her in the window. I gave her the paperwork and she gave me a SMTWTFS pillbox, a chart that showed how it was set up, and a bag of meds. She gave me the number of a psychopharmacologist named Dr. Sandy and said this is who to call for refills or if Armand seemed too down for too long, or too excited over nothing, or not sleeping, or having trouble talking or moving, or not making sense when he talked, or violent. She must have seen the look in my eyes because she said, "Just call the number if something doesn't seem right. Trust your instincts." It felt good for her to say that, although I wondered about the boy with the cowlick and if he should trust his instincts, too, if everyone, no matter how dumb, young, or crazy, should be trusting instincts. The rosy woman with her adventures, the nurse with her crazy eyes and her white uniform. There were instincts all over the place. I looked up to see my mother leaving the building. A length of toilet paper struggled to escape from her jacket pocket.

My dad said, "She sees you growing up and she's afraid of losing you."

"She said that?"

"Not exactly."

In the parking lot our car and truck were staring straight ahead like they weren't ready to talk, either. My mom's head was a rock hovering impossibly over her steering wheel. I decided to ride home with my dad because at least he was normal. I felt bad for about three seconds, putting the madman in the back for our first ride, but I enjoyed horrifying my mother by doing it. She glared at me from behind the window while she felt through her purse for her phone. Receipts, her falling-apart checkbook, an extra ring of like forty keys and I don't know if there's been forty things in her life that had locks, a separate falling-apart wallet for pictures, open dirty lifesavers and all kinds of crap that why doesn't she just throw away, like a manual for our Mister Mixer, for god's sake I've seen it in there, all these things I knew were bulging out of her purse and spilling into the car and I'm sure slid under the seat without her noticing because she was so busy glaring at me. I just hopped into the back of the truck, and my dad helped me fit my madman into his harness, which fit perfectly from what I could tell with him enveloped in his cloak. I clipped him to the tarp-ties and hopped into the cab. By that time, her car was gone. And my bag was still in there, too. I made peace with the possibility that I would sacrifice my best pants to my big day.

At first, my madman didn't seem sure how to position himself and he wouldn't put his staff down. I watched by using the mirrors so he wouldn't feel self-conscious. He definitely wobbled while we were backing up but then sat leaning against the cab and held the staff in his lap. He'd been quiet but helpful while we were fitting his harness on. I was so distracted I wasn't taking it all in, and again, I felt bad about that, but he was helping in this very gentle/unobtrusive way, letting a hand creep out from his cloak and taking a strap and then passing it back through the other side. He didn't say a thing or make a sound. I should have just put her out of my mind and really taken this opportunity, I mean it was our first impression, and as soon as we got going I felt so bad I wanted to cry for wasting it, but the thing about madmen is most of their memories are fucked up, so you never know when anything you do or don't do will stick, and they've been through so much that you kind of can't go wrong anyway, as long as you're not overall abusive or evil. As a group, they really know how to let things go, or else they'd be dead already. The truck had one of those sliding panels in the back window, so I could poke my head out every so often and see the top of his head, still hidden in his cloak, and the fabric blowing around him like a ghost but in reverse, heavy and black instead of filmy white, but still moving around as if there wasn't anyone in there when of course there was.

Then I watched my dad's head bobbing along the strip of landscape. His cheek looked really soft, even with a not-great shaving job. The plan was we'd go home and let the madman just be by himself or rest in the shed while we had dinner as a family to celebrate. Then I would bring him his plate and I guess get to know him? That's the part I hadn't done so much imagining in anticipation. I was also having my doubts about being greeted at the house with any lasagna.

"Whatever happened to your madman, Dad?" I knew it was a woman madman, and I knew it made him nervous to talk about it, and I knew he felt like he hadn't always done the right thing. I'd heard all about my mother's madmen, how she'd had one and then another and they'd both been cured, and she had a box tied with ribbons that had letters from them in it, and a certificate of appreciation from California, and invitations to come work for boards of things. The landscape was blurry and peripheral because I was looking at my dad, and I thought of the schoolhouse with the spinning weathervane out of time with everything else, and tried to remember if we'd passed it already, but I felt turned around trying to anchor myself in the recollection, and immediately after that it seemed irrelevant. Things were different, weren't they? But for some reason my dad was still hesitating the way he always had about his experiences, and I just had this sudden image of him peeling back his face, revealing his own madness, and crying out: "I'll tell you what happened to my madman! I married her!"

Instead, he winced. He said, "Honey, it's private. And very sad. And this is your big day."

I know you don't show just anyone your madman, like sex, but even people who talk all the time about something that's supposedly private are covering for something else. The more I was part of the whole adult world, the more turned out as one secret after another. My madman was still just a cloak and a stick, and oh yeah, we call him Armand. But there was my dad, who I'd supposedly known all my life, and what was he?

If the world looked different so far, the difference was it didn't look so symbolic. That is not what a girl wants when she comes of age.

At the house, my mother's car was in the driveway with its daytime running lights still on and both doors flopped open. Eyes rolled back, limbs splayed.

"Take Armand to his shed," said my father.

He was terrified.

* * *

Back in the gallery of madmen, when my mother was yelling because of what I wanted, I looked at her eyes and tried to see them objectively. Their blueness, whiteness, redness. I tried to look at her eyeballs themselves—not the lids or brow or her crow's feet or the other muscles in her face. I wanted to know how emotion could come shooting from her eyes the way it did. Maybe I couldn't block out the rest of her face, maybe that was impossible, like pretending I wasn't her kid would be impossible. Maybe the feelings came from the situation and not her body. Maybe the situation and her body were the same thing or I will never understand because I don't have enough empathy.

She said I was romanticizing. She said I'd like anyone if I knew the whole story. She said being free is not being free if you are in pain. She said madness is pain.

I said, "I have pain."

She said, "It's different for them because it's more."

What do you want to be wearing when your father comes back from checking on your mother and you learn that this time your mother has actually killed herself? This is what I wondered, sitting in the cab of the truck in the driveway, looking at the familiar world, which had become so still. Sweatpants, I thought, because you can sleep in them and be in public in them. Cross-trainers because they have good grip and breathe. Layers on top: a long-sleeved shirt under a short-sleeved shirt because it's flexible and I've seen pictures of her wearing that when I was a baby, also a fleece vest because I might have to sleep in the hospital with air conditioning, or, I kept thinking, you might have to be outside at night. I kept picturing that. Looking for her in the woods behind the house. Which one time I did do. My father was out of town and she had been crying for so many hours, I'd tried being nice, I'd tried leaving her alone, and I threatened to call dad and she said "Go ahead" in a way I took to mean if I called him, she'd finish herself off for sure. I even put my face up to hers and then screamed in a sudden burst like saying "boo!" but as loud and angry as possible and not funny. It freaked me out about myself when I screamed like that. Eventually it was like two in the morning and I was in my bed holding the phone, trying to decide what would be the moment I would call a hospital, trying to decide what the sign would be, and I heard the front door, and looked out the window, and saw her take off running into the woods. One time our cat had gone missing and years later I found her collar and her bones in the woods while I was walking, and then that night we all went into the woods to bury her, with candles, stones we'd chosen, and a baby tree, and it was beautiful. When my mother took off into the woods, I hesitated to follow her. I had this image of a beautiful candlelight thing and then just, I don't know, peace, being on my own.

But I did follow her into the woods. It was so dark but I found her curled up on the trail by a fallen mossy log. She was covered in dirt and not crying anymore. She came with me, which I don't know what I would have done if she hadn't, but for some reason I didn't even have to touch her, she just came with me. At the house she said, "Thank you for saving my life," and I let her take a bath, even though I was scared of what might happen in there, but I told myself to stop being dramatic, she was my mother and she could take a bath. Maybe I believed that I had saved her life, and that's what let me go to sleep and next day tell my father a version of it when he came home that was true but unemotional in a way that let him not make a big deal out of it and let me think it wasn't a big deal after all. But even then I knew it wasn't me that saved her life. It wasn't about me. I was just there while she was maybe going to die and maybe not, and then she just didn't.

I got out of the truck and stood in the driveway, unhooking Armand's harness. He scrambled to his feet under his cloak and used his staff of madness to steady himself on the ridged bed. I reached out my hand—the idea was he could take it and walk along to the tailgate—and there was a moment when he seemed to be deciding between dropping his stick to take my hand or not. It was impossible to know for sure with the cloak, but I had the distinct impression that he might have only one arm.

The sun was starting to set. The house was behind us. He didn't take my hand, just made his way to the end of the truck, and I lowered the tailgate, and then he sat on it. His legs dangled. I glanced to see if I could see his feet, if they would be in boots, or shoes, or sandals, or rags, or nothing. If he would have feet. But his cloak floated below them, and only the staff poked out. I hopped up onto the tailgate with him, careful not to touch him, and the truck rocked like a boat, and so, like a lookout at the prow of a ship of fools, I put my hand to my forehead and squinted toward the sun into the distance. I could spy with my little eye the roof of the shed, partway down the hill, and sparks like tiny fires in the low water in the creek, and the woods like a curtain with everything beyond darker than ever, sucking up the light. Soon the sun was setting enough that it was past the time when the pieces of the world are sharp and distinct from each other and on to when everything becomes one fuzzy mass. Our eyes saw and then didn't see the forms we knew were in there, and then saw again for a second, and then were just making it up. Okay, that's what *my* eyes were doing, anyhow. At some point I was going to have to say something to him, and if he had a voice he was probably going to say something back. Maybe something would change then. The sun was so close to set, but it hadn't set all the way. Instead of saying something, I thought about the weathervane, spinning, because I wanted the moment to last forever.

GODZILLA VERSUS THE
SMOG MONSTER

Patrick is fourteen, this is earth, it's dark, it's cold out, he's American, he's white, straight, not everyone has cell phones, he's sitting on the carpet of the TV room on the third floor holding the remote in both hands in his lap. He's sitting with one leg tucked under the other on the deep shag oval rug, his back against an enormous ottoman. Other elements of the modular sofa orbit him. It's a solid, stable position. On the second floor and on the other side of the house, behind a door off the hall that overlooks the living room, his parents sleep in a high walnut bed, under a moss green comforter. A tabby cat curls into his mother's hair. Patrick has seen his mother asleep with the cat like that, practically suctioned. Against his will, it grosses him out a little.

In the video, the Smog Monster, a wad of wet-looking gray cotton with static red eyes, has not yet met Godzilla. It hardly matters that it eventually meets Godzilla because in the end all that Patrick will remember about the movie is a scene that's not actually in the movie. It's something he figured must be happening offscreen based on the girls in their gym outfits collapsing and four men playing cards, incinerated. He remembers how the toxic, billowing Smog Monster sweeps through the sky and, as it passes between the white-gray sun and the gray-gray earth, its shadow passes over millions of people whose faces are like beads. Flesh blows from the people like sand, leaving millions of skeletons coating the hills, dead faces like the pattern in a printed fabric, a city-sized, TV-sized sheet stretched flat. He's not Jewish but he's seen old films on cable of mass Holocaust graves, and the shot he imagines could be lifted from one as a sick, low-budget solution; he pictures the Japanese filmmakers scurrying like the scientists in the movie, but with armfuls of unspooling film instead of fists of sloshing beakers. If he'd been born just a few years later, he might not even know about film. This Holocaust landscape, the bodies making a pattern you could turn into wallpaper, is what he imagines whenever there are reports of genocide coming from the kitchen radio or one of the televisions that dot the house. But later it's all blended up with this dumb video that moved him in the night.

He's wearing light blue cotton pajama bottoms and a thin sweatshirt his father wore playing hockey in college. His clavicle is incredibly delicate, poking out of the ring of the sweatshirt. Soon a professor, in subtitles, suggests that the Smog Monster rode in on a comet, a space pollution scientific freak organism. No one in Patrick's generation uses the word "ozone" to worry about the planet. Soon there's the scene where the girl's dancing on a stage in front of a multicolored projection of magnified pond scum. Patrick finds he's thinking of ice. He's picturing his father moving alone with his hockey stick across their neighbor's vast lawn that fills and freezes over every year. That afternoon he'd gone into his father's dresser for a sweatshirt and found the tape there, at the bottom of the drawer where porn ought to be. He then, in fact, set his watch for three a.m. and chose the third floor TV room instead of the living room for that very reason. Imagine, porn rising past the hallway balcony like steam, curling under the doorway and creeping under the covers to where his father lay, a man, a man with a wife and a son, with a fine, high bed, with snow-covered land, borderless and unobstructed all the way to the deep pine woods.

Instead, Patrick is watching a boy in stupid-looking high-waisted shorts follow his grandfather along the beach. The movie is so badly made that when his attention wanders for even a moment he has no idea what's going on. There are drunken Japanese hippies having visions of people turning into fish. In a long sequence, first Godzilla and then the Smog Monster stare into the screen at a series of angles. It will be years before it occurs to him that this was meant to be a dramatic show-down. He and his first real girlfriend will have broken into an abandoned grocery store. It'd been fun, racing their absurdly large carts down the emptied aisles—the absence of color, the inorganic skeleton—until he hadn't seen her in a while. He'll be running the cart through produce, wads of colored tissue and packing straw floating on the naked geometric planes of display islands, and suddenly feel done with it, the need to go at the level of panic. He'll run the cart along the tops of the aisles—dairy, beverage, cereal, frozen food, natural, ethnic, snacks, baking goods— increasingly furious because he's been texting her and texting her. *Where r u?* Finally she's way down at the other end of canned goods. She's deep in the lowest shelf, swallowed to her torso, her legs coming out of her ass in a stark V. For a second he'll think she's dead, something having shoved her in there. Then she emerges with a can held up like a torch. She says, "Look: a soup!" They lock eyes across the vast speckled lino-leum. She's so happy, and he's so angry. He thinks, *pow*. He remembers sitting secretly among furniture in the tip of a house that is pointing its nose to the moon, and above him nothing but the stratosphere.

When the movie's over Patrick brings the cassette with him to his room and slips it under the extra pillow. For a long time he tries to sleep, facing it in the dark. He tries to think about the porn he'd expected, but his thoughts keep shifting back to the crumbling bodies, the masses of them in grainy gray and ashen white. It hurts. He longs for porn, but he can't make it happen in a way that's not horrible and sick.

In the morning, kitchen sounds rise past the balcony. Patrick's window is nearly covered in frost, a vast miniature white forest, and through the ice-branches he can see his father crossing the yard in his long brown coat and over boots, using a black branch for a walking stick, poking it into the snow. He can walk on the snow for a couple of steps but then crunches through. Cold comes off the window and the sun is soft and clean. His father, alternately light and heavy, comes off as funny. Patrick pulls his feather blanket around his shoulders and shuffles downstairs in his wool socks. His mother is holding their terrier on one arm and wiggling a frying pan over the stove with the other. In the pan are three eggs, whites oval, yolks off-center in each. She's wearing a quilted bathrobe with a print-version of gingham patches. Patrick uses a foot to pull a chair out from the table and then sits in it, not really facing the table, not really facing his mother, either. He's in a beam of sunlight. He blinks and yawns. He pulls at the blanket so he's not sitting on so much of it.

"I don't think I want an egg, Mom," he says.

"Someone'll eat it. You still sleepy?" She crouches to let the terrier hop off her arm. He shakes himself as if he's wet and then leaps into Patrick's lap. Patrick holds the little dog at arm's length and it licks at the sunny air. Patrick likes the dog, but he doesn't like it to lick him, and lately the licking has been seeping into his overall opinion of the dog.

His father comes in, stamping, and then unclasps the dozen clasps on each overboot and pulls them off. He's wearing his slippers underneath, and he's got the newspaper. His mother turns the radio on and it sends out classical music. Strings. Copland?

"Brrrr. Chilly, chilly," his father says. After he hangs his coat on one of the pegs by the door he crosses to the fridge, mussing Patrick's hair as he passes by, sending the threads of dust in the sunbeam into tantrums. In a moment that no one notices, the dust plumes into the shape of the Smog Monster.

Patrick's father takes bread out and puts slices in the toaster. Soon they're all at the table. Toast, butter, jam, eggs, coffee, juice. Sometimes when Patrick comes home from school after practice or late from a game his parents will be off somewhere in the house, but at the kitchen table will be his father's briefcase on one chair and his mother's briefcase on the chair opposite it, these abbreviated versions of them, like sentries.

Three days later it's a Wednesday and at lunch Patrick and his friend Arbuckle, first name shunned and practically forgotten, get lost in conversation at the far end of the snow-covered soccer field where they like to sit on this extremely wide, ragged stump of a tree that's near the edge of the woods but not really part of the woods. They don't know it, because it's their first year at the high school, but for ages it'd been a climbing tree, and only that summer it'd been proclaimed dead enough to be dangerous. Kids used to congregate at the tree, but now it's just a stump and no one cares about it.

So Patrick and Arbuckle get to class late, starting back across the field when they hear the bell, trying to run through the snow at first but then giving up, taking it easy, trudging with their heads low, arms folded, still talking, thinking something through. Then Arbuckle heads off for French and Patrick steps into his biology class but no one even looks at him as he enters, snow pressed into shapes quietly dropping from the treads of his boots. He stops a few steps in. The room feels funny. They're all watching the television on its wheeled cart. It sits at the front of the rows of one-armed desks, and Mr. Bernard is sitting in Patrick's—in the second row, watching. News is on. There's footage of raging, raging fire. It's raging in a box in the upper-right of the screen. Patrick's seen commercials for a videotape of fire you can play to make your television more festive—he and Arbuckle joked about buying it for his uptight parents, ages ago, when they saw it in a dollar bin. But they didn't buy it because after they thought of it, the joke was over.

This fire, however, is a real fire, raging in the city of Los Angeles. Something swooped overhead and dropped, or dropped something. Something fell burning from the sky and what is it, chemicals, flaming viruses, maybe nuclear—whatever it is, California is burning on the television and burning across the country. There's also no way to tell how far away the video is being shot from because looking at fire up close is pretty much the same as looking at fire far away, as long as it fills the screen. "My country," people say on the TV, anchors and men on the street. "Our country."

Patrick stays in his spot on the periphery. All around the room are posters of biology things. Definitive drawings of cross-sections of plants and animals. Everyone listens to the reporters, watching the fire. Landmarks are gone forever, museums and mansions enumerated by one after another correspondent. A series of explosions level the hills. One of Mr. Bernard's hands is clinging to the slender arm of Patrick's desk. He has a round head, glasses, and strings of black hair that his scalp shows through. He's got a quirk of smoothing his hand across them. He's about the same height and build as Patrick, and while Patrick has tried to picture the lives of some other teachers, he has never even thought about Mr. Bernard except in terms of biology. Now that Mr. Bernard is in his spot, Patrick follows the teacher's eyes to the intercom, back to the television, then back to the intercom. The speaker is dangling from its wires in a corner near the ceiling over the blackboard, but everyone knows it's done nothing but occasionally spit for months. Mr. Bernard's homeroom just does the pledge on their own. Notes come from the office, if anything. If Patrick moved to the front of the room, that could complete a kind of reversal, and the thought comes close but doesn't actually cross his mind. He stays by the door. He is looking at Mr. Bernard for some ideas of what to think, but meanwhile Mr. Bernard's mind is filled with the fire and includes Patrick only as a sort of pixel among many student-pixels massed over time. He's an okay teacher who occasionally, maybe every few years, gets swept up in a kid. He'll find himself thinking about the kid's life, and trying to do something to help the kid, and have to pull himself back.

The reporter they're watching gets a message in her ear to move farther from the billowing fire, and when she sends it back to the anchor Mr. Bernard says, "We'll wait and there'll be an announcement." None of the kids are saying anything, but two girls link fingers across the aisle. Outside, it's snowing again. Patrick lets his backpack slip to the floor and into the puddle from his boots. After a while Mr. Bernard says, "I have an announcement," but then the news anchor says something about the fires raging into San Diego, Santa Barbara, about speculations, who is responsible, and he doesn't say anything.

In the doorway, Patrick remembers another emergency with Mr. Bernard, back in September. One of the kids in their class had tried to kill himself by taking all the prescriptions he scrounged up in his house. It was supposed to be assembly where everyone processed together, and that had already happened, but the kid had been in their biology class before the coma, and the girl who had been his partner in collecting specimens had been assigned to join another group, making a threesome. In class, the girl kept saying, "It's just not going to be the same." It came off a little like she was complaining about the group, and after about the third time she said it, Mr. Bernard lost his temper. Patrick had never seen a teacher lose his temper like that. He said, "Hold it, listen up, class," and then just went off. He was grasping a wooden yardstick for some reason. He wore such ridiculous plaid pants no one could tell if they were an intentional joke, but Patrick saw him shake, and in the doorway he remembers being afraid the man was going to cry, praying and praying his teacher wouldn't cry. He remembers this vibrating hope against hope, he remembers not what Mr. Bernard said but how angry it made him to see his teacher out of control like that, and then the memory dives back under the surface and his mind doesn't hook onto it again.

Mr. Bernard will always remember what he said. He said, "I know you're all freaking out and excited. I know it feels like this changes everything, and I know half of you are thinking that might be cool, even necessary. But let me tell you, I know several of you in this very room have experienced some real hardship. And some of you are going to learn very soon what tragedy is if you don't know it already. That, my friends, is life," he said. He dropped the yardstick accidentally and it made a huge smack hitting the floor. He'd been teaching for twenty years. He'd talked to kids whose parents beat each other, who were sick, dying, kids whose parents fucked them when they were babies. He'd had a refugee kid who never spoke, whose eyes rested only on the things between people, and who the fuck knows what happened in the world to do that to her. "I am here to tell you that nothing is changed," he'd said that day. "Ice ages come and go. Stars supernova and nothing is changed. Species go extinct every day. So you can take heart in that." After school, Patrick had said something to Arbuckle about Mr. Bernard losing it in class and never thought of it again until now. In fact, three months later and the school is pretty used to one of them being off in a coma. It's what Mr. Bernard might call resilience.

"I have to go home," Mr. Bernard says, sick of it, rising from Patrick's desk and returning to his own. "If you want to stay, I'll stay here if you want me to stay, but otherwise I'm going."

Busses aren't around, the parking lot is crazy, and Patrick gets a ride with a senior who lives on his street. Sara has a lot of light brown, almost golden fluffy hair, and even though she's not a big deal at the school, she doesn't usually say anything to him. Their parents know each other, but even as children, Sara and Patrick never got along. It's no loss either way. Practically all he knows about her is that she's adopted and she's part black. Biracial, which sounds like a part of an insect. Multiethnic, which sounds like a ride at a carnival. Sara's got a black Trans Am with a red interior—not the kind of car most kids go for in this district in this moment in history—and her hair really stands out against it. Her eyes are sunken and blurry, and while some kids look a little dazed, and some kids are running around like they're high on sugar, Sara has clearly been crying. Maybe she knows someone in California. Patrick has an older cousin who lived in Santa Cruz for a while but now he's back.

Her hair rises in the wind in one fluffy mass.

"You okay?" he says. Her hair looks like the Smog Monster, and while it's true that he doesn't like her, it's such a juvenile thought he pushes it aside.

"This is all so very fucked up," Sara says, shaking her head. She's being nice, that's one thing being stripped and raw can make you, is nice, but he's skeptical. He thinks she's so immersed in what she's feeling that she's assuming everyone feels exactly like her and that's what makes her be so nice. She's feeling her commonality with all humankind, and it doesn't matter what he feels.

They're rising and falling along the slick, curving road. Long rows of evergreens line some of the properties, and acres of snow separate the road from the houses it leads to. There's an old donkey who lives with a pony in a post-and-rail paddock with a little wooden shelter. When they pass the paddock, the donkey is lying in the snow, curled like a dog on a hearth, and the pony is standing over it. Gray donkey, white pony, dark rail fence, pale, pale sky.

Sara wants to drive him right up to his house, she insists on it, but it's a very long driveway and though it's plowed, it's icy. They have an extremely grown-up-sounding conversation, a kind of I'll-get-the-check, no-no-I'll-get-the-check exchange, over whether or not she should drive all the way down the driveway. Patrick wins by saying he wants to get the mail and when he gets out he just says, "Thanks. Really Sara, the walk will do me good," which completely freaks him out for a second, like the remark comes directly from the future. He gets the mail but instead of walking down the driveway, he uses his father's footprints across the loping yard. They're left from days ago, iced over and just that one set.

Inside, Patrick's parents are upstairs in their bed on the green comforter in their work clothes, watching California burn on TV. Their shoes are in the hall, empty and at odd angles, as if the people in them had disintegrated mid-step. When Patrick arrives in the doorway, his parents hold out their arms and he gets up into the high walnut bed with them. Patrick's mother shifts so that he can share the green pillow she's leaning on. He can smell that she's had a cigarette. The cat's in his father's lap, her tail dripping over onto Patrick's leg, shifting like a hunting snake. The terrier hops up and his mother distracts it from the cat by nudging it playfully with her feet. The terrier bites at her toes and then lies down, leaning into the curves of her arches. The TV continues its coverage. The fire is spreading. It's past Fresno. It's consuming the state but has yet to cross over its lines. Suspects accumulate, worldwide. The anchor chokes up, waxes and relates. Sometimes Patrick's father offers an analysis and sometimes his mother offers an analysis. They talk about who could have done it, who in the world. Patrick points to the map on the television and says things like, "I didn't know that country was pronounced like that. I think that lady said it wrong. Is it bigger or smaller than, say, Kansas?" Or he asks, "Is stocking up dumb? Are we stocked up?"

But mostly he finds he's feeling wonderful and warm, there between his parents, with the cat and the dog. It's such a big and carefully furnished house for there to be so many lives in those few square feet of space. He thinks, *I am in the moment.* Nothing is dirty. Everything is either very near or very far. The fan turns overhead, pushing heated air down.

At ten p.m., Patrick is already in his bed, reading by the light of a little clip-on book light that came with a magazine subscription. It's cheap and the bulb doesn't fit right in its socket. The light keeps flickering. His father is upstairs in the TV room, still watching the coverage.

They'd eaten cheese sandwiches for dinner, in his parents' room, a picnic on the comforter. They thought about ordering pizza, but no one wanted to go wait at the end of the driveway. His mother cried for a while. "Your whole generation is shot," she said to Patrick, and then tried to take it back. Patrick cried a little, too, at this idea of being part of a generation, but also because his mother was crying. She'd taken her suit jacket off and had her bathrobe on over her blouse and trousers. She fell asleep like that, among them. He wanted to talk it all through with Arbuckle, but because Arbuckle's family resists technology as harmful, they have only one telephone and one telephone line. When Patrick called, Arbuckle said they weren't allowed to tie it up. He said they had people in California.

Now, in bed, Patrick's reading a superhero comic, one from years ago when he used to read them all the time. In this one, the main superhero girl is losing control of her powers, they're just getting way out of hand. She's hovering in space about to destroy an entire planet and she can't stop herself. The bulb in his tiny lamp is flickering and then, just as she's sure her head will explode, a soft beam of light slides in and out of his window and he hears a far-off impact. He gets to his knees and looks out the window. Far across the yard and up at the road at the end of the driveway there's a streetlamp, and the lamp shines a diffuse oval on the ground. The black road and the snow divide the lit space. There's a car in the light, crossing the line. Patrick gets his glasses from the night table and then he can see that the car has crashed into the mailbox. The silver mailbox itself is in the yard, shining in the car's headlights, and the head-lights stretch toward the house like the antennae of a bug from another world.

He listens for his father or mother to respond in some way, but they don't. He puts on his slippers and pulls a big wool sweater on over the pajamas and sweatshirt he's been wearing to bed every night. Then he trots across the landing and peeks into his parents' room. His mother is there, still asleep. He trots upstairs far enough to hear the television still going, a newsperson interviewing a rescuer just off his shift, the sound of the fire like static behind their voices.

At the kitchen door he takes his father's overboots and clasps the clasps over his slippers and the legs of his pajamas. He puts on a hat, a brown one with earflaps and strings, as if you'd ever tie them under your chin. He takes a flashlight from the utility closet and stuffs a pair of gloves into his waistband, but as soon as he steps outside, the cold smacks him hard enough that he puts them on. The driveway is densely iced so he jogs at the edge, where at least there are crumbled pieces for traction, but still he slips twice, catching himself on the snow bank. Even before he recognizes the car, he recognizes the fuzzy cloud of hair over the steering wheel. He's worried for a second that he's about to encounter something he's not prepared for, something that could change his life. *If her face is gone*, he thinks, *if I lift her hair and she has no face....*

But Sara raises her head and her face is intact, puffy though. She watches him approach and opens the car door as he nears. She shifts in her seat, putting her feet on the snow. He doesn't come all the way up to her. She's still older, she's still a senior, and even though he's feeling a softness toward her, part of him knows it'll be short-lived because she is, after all, okay.

"So, you're okay?" he says.

"Do you think it'll go?"

He crunches a few steps around to the front of the car and there's a place in its nose that's pretty smushed. Still, the hood is down and intact, and although the bumper is twisted and part of it's come undone, it's not blocking anything that he can see. Part of the post that held the mailbox is sort of impaling it, between the body and the bumper, coming up across the radiator grille, which is bent back to accommodate it. If the post doesn't hold to the ground, though, he thinks the car ought to go.

"Want me to try to back it out?"

"It's my car, Patrick." It's a rebuke, and he almost snaps back at her, something about leaving his warm bed, but when he looks at her through the windshield the expression on her face stops him, and he watches her hear herself, and change her mind. Then she says, "Why don't you get in? If we can get it going, I'll show you something."

He gets in. The car backs out pretty much immediately. He pulls the brake and then gets out and looks with his flashlight. The mailbox post is still wedged up there, but when he looks under the car, the end of it hovers over the pavement maybe half a foot. He gets back in. "I think it'll be okay," he says. "But go slow."

"Fuck it," Sara says.

They go fast, but he's not scared. Her face is lit by the green glow of the instrument panel and it strikes him what a baby face she has. It's a little thrilling, the turn things have taken, driving away from the house in the night. If it was Arbuckle, he'd have some pot, but if it was Arbuckle, they wouldn't have a car.

Patrick doesn't remember it, but the way his family met Sara's was that when they'd first moved into the house, back when Patrick was seven, Sara's parents came over. "It was so nice," Patrick's mother said when she mentioned it to Patrick. This was around when he started middle school and was worried about all the kids he knew from elementary who wouldn't be there, and all the kids he didn't know who would. He'd asked what it was like when they first moved into the neighborhood, after his father finished his degrees and finally had a real salary. Sara and her family were minor characters in his mother's story about fitting in—it was their first real place, she said, a place of their own, but his family had roots here and hers did not, so it was a little uneven-feeling at first. Sara's parents came over when there were still boxes everywhere. Patrick had pictured a dumpy mom in a kind of summery dress with strawberries on it, and a gray father in a warped fedora, holding a casserole with silver potholders. His mother said, "When I saw them, I thought, what a nice neighborhood this must be. But then they gave us flyers from their church and it didn't seem like they were just being nice anymore." Still, after it turned out that Patrick's mother represented her company when it was a client of Sara's father's department at his company, sometimes the couples paired up at social functions, and a few times when Patrick's family had a party, Sara's family came. Once, they set up a buffet in the living room and Patrick and Sara watched from the balcony. Sara got bored quickly, and took her book to the third-floor TV room. Patrick stayed watching. He was ten, maybe eleven. From above, the grown-ups really did look like aliens, in their shiny clothing. Their arms were coming right out of their heads, the little nubs of their feet poking out the edges of their pant legs.

"I was going to California," says Sara. Her hair glows warmly around her face in the black-green light. "Not tonight—I'll show you where I was going tonight. But the whole idea was to graduate and then get the fuck to California."

"You know people there?"

"No," she says, annoyed. "I mean yes, like I have aunts there, and they have progeny. But I was going besides that." She shakes her head as if that will get rid of being annoyed, but then stops, and he thinks it must hurt from the crash. "I mean, I don't care if those people are there. It's such a big place. It never even mattered that they were there. I could just go, you know, oranges, sunshine. Better people. I was going to go there and change my life, and now it's gone."

"Are you an actress?" he says, instead of asking if these are real biological aunts she's talking about, which is what he wants to know.

"Fuck no. Jesus, Patrick, don't you have any imagination?"

He can't believe she has the power to hurt him, but when she says this, she does. He hears static. Even though he plays soccer, Patrick primarily pegs himself as an imaginative person. He reads a lot of pulp sci-fi novels, but he also reads a lot of books on history, intellectual things. He thinks of himself as an imaginative person in a school full of unimaginative people. A town of them, too. A whole world. But when Sara accuses him, he can see, for a second, like a door opening in a room so dark you never knew there was a door, how he has no imagination at all.

Sara makes a fairly wild turn and the car slides a bit before settling into a more controlled bumping across the icy gravel road. "Don't you want to know where we're going?"

He waits for her to go ahead and tell him, but she doesn't, so then he says, "Yes." She raises and lowers her eyebrows, something he can't really see but still manages to picture is happening. When she still doesn't answer, he thinks quickly and then says, "No."

It turns out it's a cave, and Patrick will not forget it.

They'd parked the car. They brought his flashlight. They pushed through bare thorny bushes to a tractor path so deep in sealed snow it could be a frozen creek. They hardly broke through at all. Somewhere in their American history, Patrick's family owned a lot of land, and he wondered if they might have owned these woods, these mountains. In the darkness the side of a mountain rose. As they walked, the mountain shifted from brush-covered and snow-buried mulch to stony walls and what actually *was* a frozen creek running along it. Sara took his arm, the one not holding the flashlight, pulled him down the embankment, and they crossed the frozen creek. It was cold, but with no wind, so not cold enough to hurt. When they came to the cave he hardly knew he was in it until she had him seated on a mound of pine needles.

He shines the flashlight around, and when the beam hits her eyes they flash yellow. He tells himself she's a girl, not an animal, but he can't help it—it's a cave, she's immersed in it, and her eyes flashed. He can't tell what she's doing—touching the walls, looking for something she left?

"Cool," he says. "I didn't know there were caves out here." It's a small enough space that it seems stupid to ask if they can make a fire, but he asks anyway. "I know, I know," he says, laughing. "But it's a cave. I had to ask."

"No," she says. He can hear her smiling. "We can have a fire." She makes a fire right outside the opening, so the smoke has somewhere to go but they can still catch some heat. It's amazing that she can, that in the middle of snow she can just shove around and gather enough branches. She uses a cigarette lighter from her pocket, and a twisted-up receipt. It was dry before it snowed, and now that the snow's frozen, the twigs hiss and pop but get it going fine.

Again, he feels cozy. He can't help it. California is burning, the fire gobbling Eureka, all that marijuana up in smoke, people and animals are dying, the air is poisoned, the ocean is boiling, fishes making for Hawaii as fast as their flippers will carry them, rock tops exploding from sea cliffs like missiles, and he feels cozy, trying to figure out if maybe he's attracted to Sara. He knows the one about how people have sex in the last moments before the end of the world, but it doesn't feel like the end of the world. Is that why he doesn't feel like he ought to be having sex? She has that black car, and she built a fire for him, and they're in a cave in the night in woods that suddenly feel like his own. Nice contained crackling little shadowcasting world. Her puffy face is so soft-looking and her hair comes out of her hat like clouds from behind a sun. She takes her hat off and shakes the hair. Patrick takes off his overboots and sits there on his pine needles in his slippers in the cave, feeling at home. He holds his hat in his lap and ties and unties the earflap strings.

It strikes him that he doesn't have to go back, not if he doesn't want to. Lately Arbuckle has been becoming a Marxist. When Patrick said, "So you want to kill millions of people and make everyone poor?" Arbuckle said, "Marxism is a critique of capitalism." Then when Patrick asked his father about it, his father laughed. He said, "Tell Arbuckle to let me know when he comes up with a better system," and when Patrick went back to Arbuckle with that, Arbuckle said, "Not to disrespect your dad, but you don't have to have all the answers to think there's a problem, you just have to think there might be a better way."

In the cave Patrick thinks, *But I like my home.*

"How's it been at your house?" he asks Sara. He's shining his flashlight around the space, sweeping the light along the walls. There's not much space to cover but still, it feels like what he's doing is sweeping, covering the space in a methodical way, the way a scenting dog covers a field.

"Dad's out of town. Mom worked late because everyone went home. She likes the office quiet. She said keep a list of who calls to say they're okay."

"Harsh," Patrick says.

"I guess she's upset but you'd never know it. She says work is therapeutic. And otherwise you let them win. She says, gotta put food on the table. I hate therapy."

"Like you're going to starve."

"I know, really." Then she says, "I don't think just sitting here is moral." She's saying words off-hand, but he has never seen anyone so stripped as she seems to be right now. She's phasing in and out as he moves the light. Her hair keeps reminding him of things. The Smog Monster, of course. Then with the hat it reminded him of fried eggs. Now it's the most silent explosion in history.

He keeps moving the light from the flashlight along the walls. It's hard to see past its dim concentric circles to the rock itself. It's impossible to tell what color anything is. He thinks about how it feels in his bed in the dark, the house like a layer cake, like geographic time. He thinks about generation after generation. Sometimes his parents say "When this house is yours," and sometimes they say "The world is your oyster," or "When you leave the nest." Meanwhile, beyond what Patrick will ever know, Sara's having a fantasy. She's running through a field of dry summer wheat with a guiding moon, holding a lantern high, near her head. Within the lantern's light is only wheat, her head, her invisible pounding heart, but her mind is reaching. In her other hand, she's carrying a message with a wax seal. It's something she expects to have to eat once it's delivered. She's wearing a billowing white shirt and a leather vest that laces up the front. The fantasy takes place during the Revolutionary War. Or it's a vision of the future.

At some point, Patrick realizes he's been looking, all this time, sweeping the walls, for ancient drawings.

They stay in their round little cave and look at their little half-in, half-out fire. The harder they look at the fire, the closer it seems to get. At some point Sara notices that for one thing, she's basically trapped them in the cave. If something came from behind, like a wild animal, they'd have to go through the fire to get out. But there's nothing behind them except the back of the cave. Something would have to come to life from nothing in order to get them.

Two weeks and two days later California is kaput. It's a heaving, flattened, blowing, billowing mass of ash and soot and toxicity. It's Saturday morning, and Patrick's parents are eating breakfast side by side in bed, kind of an ordeal because they had to go downstairs, make it, and then carry it up on trays. The cat and the terrier are off somewhere, hunting. Patrick comes in with a cup of coffee and sits in the walnut armchair between the door and their bed, sipping. He has a clear view of the room, the antiques that furnish it, his mother and father floating among comforters, the line of their sight that leads to the news. The television beams steadily from a converted armoire with shutters poised like wings to contain it. Televisions should be popping and fizzling out all over town, but they are inexhaustible.

Sara's gone. After the cave, Patrick had felt bright and awake but she was sleepy so he drove the black car. He had never driven a car with a sleeping person in it. Along the way, the post fell from its nose and rattled to the side of the road. At the top of his driveway, he stopped the car and had a few moments of looking at Sara. He touched her right where the edge of her sweater met her neck, to wake her up. Then they both got out, crossed paths wordlessly, and she took her place in the driver's seat.

She yawned. She said, "The snow's pink," and then drove away.

A few days later her parents called his parents. Patrick listened on the TV room extension. Now it's two weeks and she still hasn't been back to school, just hijacked the disaster for him and disappeared. The parents think she's gone looking for her real family. Her mother's reported it to the police. She's making posters. She said, "We tried to give her stability in this crazy world."

Patrick keeps expecting the disappearance to show up on the news, but he can't even remember if this is the kind of thing that would be news before California. He keeps having dreams they're in the cave, that it's the end of the world and he's seducing her. He can't help it. Things get pretty pornographic. Now, now, now, she says. Now, now. No. Now. Sometimes there are cave drawings on the wall of horses and buffalo, arrows flying, and sometimes the drawings come to life and trample them with delicate massaging hooves while they're fucking. Why is it surprising, he wonders, that drawings made of outlines, drawings that are translucent, worn over thousands of years, have almost no weight? Why is he so sure they ought to be able to kill him?

He tried to talk everything through with Arbuckle at lunch on the tree stump at school, surrounded by old snow. Footprints were everywhere, even though there was no reason for anyone to go out in the field. He tried not to do what he's seen boys like him do in movies, movies that he can't tell if they're about him or making fun of him. He didn't say, "She was hot and I could of fucked her," the way he would in one of those movies. He said, "She took me to a cave, and I felt like I was moving through time."

Arbuckle said, "If she didn't get kidnapped it's irresponsible to take off like that."

Patrick felt his insides grow taut, heat up. "That's bullshit," he said. "One thing about Sara, she's deep." He knows California doesn't exist, but the way he imagines it, that's still where she's gone. He knows the coast is a soup of ash and mud from what's left of the ocean, but he still thinks of her there, swooping over this primordial glop, as if to witness the emergence of something like a whole new planet, as if she could be the one creating whatever will become of it.

"Deep or stupid," Arbuckle said, like this happened every day. Patrick couldn't believe it. He kept looking at Arbuckle and thinking, *Is this my generation?* Arbuckle kept talking. He explained how the secret money behind the government did it to California and was trying to put the blame all over the map. "It's our own damn fault," he said, solemnly. "We did it to ourselves."

"Did what?" Patrick yelled. "You're fine. Sara's gone!"

"Where the hell did all this Sara come from?" Arbuckle yelled back. "All you ever talk about anymore is Sara."

Patrick said nothing. He just stared at Arbuckle as if they were at opposite ends of the vast white field.

Not to mention, the kid from their class still hasn't woken up, doesn't know a thing about any of it.

Back home in the armchair, Patrick is watching his mother trying to keep the tray balanced on her knees as she maneuvers her butter knife into the butter. Folded and refolded sections of newspaper bob in the green waves of the comforter. The television pursues its intrigues. He pictures himself and the TV both in orbit around his parents in their bed. He zeroes in on his father, who seems to be growing a beard.

"Dad," he says, "Did you know there's a debate on the internet about whether Godzilla is a boy or a girl?"

"No, I did not know that," he says.

"Did you know that Godzilla was born of U.S. atrocities perpetrated against Japan but by the seventies turned into the defender of Tokyo?"

"I may," says his father, "have been vaguely aware." He gives his focus to Patrick. "Why?"

"Well," Patrick says, "because I've been wondering: how come you have *Godzilla Versus the Smog Monster* hidden in your sweater drawer?"

Patrick's mother laughs and puts down her knife. "You have *Godzilla Versus the Smog Monster* hidden in your sweater drawer?"

"What are you doing in my sweater drawer?" asks his father. Patrick plucks at the front of the hockey sweatshirt, to point it out. "Oh," says his dad, and goes back to his muffin. "I used to love that sweatshirt," he says. Goofy crumbs tumble.

"No, Dad, really," says Patrick. "A person doesn't just hide things for no reason." Somewhere in the night he made a decision that if he wanted to say something, he'd just say it, given the circumstances. There's an umbrella leaning against the side of the chair, and half-consciously, Patrick picks it up and holds it in his lap. Across the room, his father's face shifts—it's not a shadow falling over, not a sudden light in his eyes, there isn't something inside him trying to get out, not anything like that. All it is, is his father looks frightened, truly frightened, just for a moment, but in a way that he has never seen before in his father, or perhaps anyone. Then he recovers. He looks at his son, and he says, "I forgot."

"Come on, honey," says his mother. "Why do you have *Godzilla*

Versus the Smog Monster hidden in your sweater drawer? After all these years," she says to Patrick, winking, "it's good to know we still have mystery."

"I forgot," his father insists, and this time Patrick doesn't believe him, not for a second. He knows the one about the boy realizing his father is not so strong and wise after all, is maybe even a cheat, a crook, a scoundrel. He finds that the umbrella he's holding has shifted in his grasp so that it's pointing at the bed, and the way he's holding it, he's shocked to notice, is like he's holding his dick. He pushes it off his lap and then reaches down and picks it up again. He wonders what to do with it, and then puts it back exactly where it was before, leaning against the side of the chair.

On one wall of the bedroom is a hunt print, painted by a once-famous painter for Patrick's great-grand-someone, depicting land that used to be in the family. Horses and dogs leap a log, no fox in sight. Across from it there's a gilt-framed botanical, the kind that shows how a plant goes from seed to seeding. Who knows where that came from. They echo, wall to wall. His mother is propped on her elbow, curled up a little, gazing into the ashes on TV.

"It's so weird," his father says. He stares at a correspondent who is standing on the edge of Nevada.

"Really Dad, it doesn't matter."

"What?" says his father.

"Never mind," says Patrick. There's his father, lost, as if lost in a vast tundra. It's the first time Patrick's looked at his father and really seen himself there, in the past and the future at once. It shakes him. It makes a little dust rise. He tries to think of reasons to hide a video, other than what's recorded on it—ways it could be symbolic as an object. He thinks, *Something he watched when he cheated on my mother.* He thinks, *Something he never watched because the day he rented it he embezzled money at work and got away with it ever since.* And that's the limit of his imagination. For years, when he dreams embarrassing dreams of Sara, she's the Smog Monster, swooping over hills and valleys, a friendly toxic pollution freak from outer space. But one day when he's a man, out there living in a freezing city, such as it is, working at a job, playing in a band at least for now, he looks out his window through the frost forest and what he sees, finally, does not feel like land that is his or belongs to him in any way.

A HUNDRED
APOCALYPSES

I.
A QUARTER OF A
HUNDRED APOCALYPSES

hands out for a new future

FRESH

After so many people were washed away by the disasters, there was usually someone outside the grocery store with a collection bucket. On a sunny day I biked over, feeling good. I walked around the grocery store, especially the produce islands, feeling pretty good about my choices and my healthy way of life. Nobody is mentioning how the increasing rate of madness is apocalyptic. It's because we mostly eat corn. There are so many decisions to be made in the grocery, that cold room of consciousness. But tell you the truth, I kept asking for it. I was asking for the apocalypse. I was tired of the way things were going. I was looking forward to fresh everything. With the slate wiped clean, the whole world would be at my beck and call. Anything could be around the corner, I thought, pushing my cart through the grocery air. There was the aisle of condiments. There were the pyramids of newfangled soup. Everything that would have happened in the event could really be a turning point for me.

CAKE

She baked an angel food cake for the dinner party, which means it's as white as is possible in cake except golden on the outside and you have to cut it with a serrated knife. It's funny to eat because you can kind of tear it, unlike most cakes. It stretches a little. It's a little supernatural, like an angel.

I was watching her with her boyfriend because I admire them and am trying to make them an example in my life of good love being possible. Toward the end of the cake everyone was talking and a couple of people were seeing if they could eat the live edible flowers that she'd put on the cake for decoration. A fairy cake. She told a story about making the cake. There wasn't a lot left. Everyone was eating the ends of their pieces in different ways, and because of the stretchy texture there were more methods than usual, and no crumbs at all.

Really funny cake.

I tried to imagine making the cake, same as I often tried to imagine love. I would never make a cake. So it's down to, say, less than a quarter of the cake and the boyfriend reaches across the table—it's a big table that no one else would be able to reach across, he just has really long arms, and he takes the serrated knife, but when he cuts at the cake he doesn't do the sawing action, he just presses down, which defeats the point of a serrated knife. The cake squishes as he cuts it in half; it was only a piece of itself already, clinging to its imaginary axis, and now it's not even a wedge—it's pushed down like you can push down the nose on your face—and then he takes his piece with his hands and I watch the last piece of cake to see if it'll spring back up but it doesn't, it's just squished on one side like someone stepped on it.

But here's what I don't understand, is how all through it she's just chatting with the dinner guests and it's like he's done nothing at all. She's not looking at him like "You squished the cake!" and she's not looking at him like "He loves the cake so much he couldn't help himself," and he doesn't seem to be thinking "Only I can squish the cake!" Or is he?

I never know how to read people.

But here's what else: watching the round cake disappear, watching the people trying to make the most of their pieces, people coveting the cake on one hand and reminding themselves on the other that this will not be the last cake. But will it be the last? I look at their love and I feel like this could be the very last piece of it on earth, and just look at it.

WANTING

All day he filled his eyes with explosions and commercials. At night he walked through the fanciest part of the neighborhood: blinds crossing vast windows, enormous foyers, each with one shining fixture suspended like the only planet in the universe of one house after another, expanses of plaster, vaulted ceilings, the geometries of staircases, rugs on walls. Automatically his mind unified with want. More flowers, more pottery, better furniture, less dirt, excellent collections of film through history, tailored clothing, quality craftsmanship, the cutting edge, caring so much, the fluffy covers, the beauty, the rich. No wonder televisions hunched behind louvered cabinet doors, sniffing through the slats, their pissed mouths shut. He walked to get his head out of the war, and walking worked. Why, why, why? One day he'd been wondering, and then, walking, wanting everything he saw is what explained it all. Then he was back where he started, in the cul de sac in the cosmos between the news and the body. Next door, his neighbor's silver rowboat was beached in the cactus garden. It gleamed in the street-lit night, appearing as shards. Like anything else, the thing about an apocalypse is it can't go on forever, and this is what saves it and saves us in the end. Sure, not everyone, but I mean us in general.

For some months nothing would do to eat except bread, any kind, including biscuits, croissants, dinner buns, hoagie rolls, Irish soda, artisan peasant, challah, brioche, lavash, pugliese, baguette full, demi, sweet, sour, marble, pita, vegan, Wonder or whatever grain, any of a zillion crackers, which sounds like a decent amount to eat except that bread was it, and it was nothing but bread. She tried to find other things to eat. She searched her cookbooks and then the last of the phone books, imagining meals. Woe on the sofa, woe on the stairs. She went out and walked around town, reading menus, her pockets heavy with cash. She took the train into the city where guys in red jackets or bowties stood in the street outside their restaurants, took her by the elbow, and described the food they could give her. Her head, like someone else's stomach, filled with meals. She let the ideas of them accumulate in piles before her, multicolored, glistening, weighting her utensils, stopping at her teeth. Then she went home and ate bread, hating it, and hating ending up with one and then another piece of Christ, slice of life, hunk of flesh, daily shut the fuck up about bread. Bread, the least common denominator of food. The earth carried everything else like condiments, like lace, like prefixes and suffixes. Then one day. Then one day. Then one day.

OPTIONS

A. MANY

A little man with enormous glasses in a floppy green hat and a blue rain slicker has placed himself on an orange stepladder eye-to-knots with a dormant tree in front of the arched entrance to his mouse-colored house, raising a yellow hacksaw, sizing it up for pruning, which he's clearly always doing; it's pared to the shape of a candelabra, bare knuckles, *he has made its history*. The bones of a cathedral, the inside of a whale, architectures of bodies, buildings, heavens enclosing earth, some god on a stepladder, composing, friendly, the sky one density of gray, his froggy, neighborly smile among colors, as if nothing else in the world matters.

B. HALF

Or a drawing I remember from an exhibit of the works of madmen: the pencil lines of half a city, one line for the sidewalk extending horizontally, like a sidewalk or a plank from the truncated SkYlInE_____, a line moving rightward into the blank page, like time.

THREAT

For years, a telephone pole leaned, a fear at the back of the neighborhood. That evening they went home and poured several very even trays of ice cubes. I was dressed for the apocalypse. I was depressed for the apocalypse. I carried a bundle of dust like a nest. My heart beat in its fleshy pocket. Girls sketched one another in an auditorium. Worms had tried to make it across our porch overnight and now they lay like something shredded, like shredded bark, but deader. My friends, looking ashen, kept waiting for the telephone. An iris wilted into a claw. A bathtub sunk in our vast yard. New birds gathered like, I don't know, a lack of entropy?

PUPPET

When she speaks to me in the voice of her dog, do I answer the dog? A guy who worked with me at the store was trying to make it as a puppeteer. We had a party at his house for our manager, Linda, who was leaving, and she brought two white terriers with her for beer and cake. We gathered as if for a group photo, facing the empty sofa. Eric got out his puppets and crouched behind it. These were hand-puppets in the shapes of a donkey and a fish. Then the donkey and the fish came up from behind it. Eric was a good puppeteer, and the donkey and fish were funny, but what was funniest was Linda's puppet-sized dogs, who sat in the front row and were completely taken in by the magic. They followed with their heads like in tennis. You could see how excited they were to find out what would happen next. After all, *I* want to know what will happen next. I want to know what will happen if I look at you while you're talking as if you are your dog and talk back to you as if I'm—I don't know, what could I talk to you like? Anything?

THE CYCLE OF LIFE

She really needed some time off work so she took maternity leave, but the baby was so much work it was like she wasn't getting any time off at all, so she killed the baby (hold on, hold on…) and that gave her time off for grieving, a whole other hell of work plus the guilt, and by the time she started to recover she had to go back to work, but pretty soon the future seemed so stupid she started wanting a baby again. When she looked into her options, one that apparently a zillion people had chosen and she hadn't even known about was a move to the trash-heaps of Navarro. That put things in perspective. No, she thought, my options are way more limited than that, thank the good lord above. She felt her back against the warm wall of her office. She felt her cells battling it out below-deck. She ate a stale pastry. She had one more idea. It was like an egg in her brain waiting to go off.

JULY FOURTH

Got there and the ground was covered with bodies. Lay down with everyone and looked at the sky, bracing for the explosions.

QUESTIONS IN SIGNIFICANTLY
SMALLER FONT

I have some questions I would like to pose regarding the End Times. Why disguise angels as aliens? Is the pope the Antichrist? Is date setting okay? Who are the 144,000? Is the millennium literal or figurative? Is the United States of America in Bible prophesy? Does End Time render stewardship of the Earth irrelevant? Will there be a partial Rapture? Will the Lord provide until Jesus returns? What is the marriage supper of the Lamb? Does what's happening in Israel today mean the End Times are quickly approaching? What is the abomination of desolation? What about the weather? Which time zone is the real time zone? What about the economy and capitalism in general? Is the Devil working overtime? What are tribulation saints? Can the Mark of the Beast be accepted by mistake? Who came up with the EU? What is a red heifer? How long is a generation? Can you lose your eternal rewards? How do we know the Tribulation will last seven years? I am afraid of the end of the world and yet I long for it. Why? What will the apocalypse mean for narrative? What will it mean for Haiti, I mean now? Boy, you know, I have some more questions. Is there a Palestinian people? When will God invade? If Jesus is God, why was He unable to do certain things while on Earth? Was He nailed through His palm or His wrist? Are there different kinds of speaking in tongues? À la languages? Explain about parables and why couldn't He just say what He meant? Did tombs break open and dead people walk the Earth? I am unmarried and thirty. Why? Is having money a bad thing? When does Daylight Savings Time begin and end? Is it possible to win the War on Terror? Are horoscopes real? What is the difference between white and black magic? Is genetic research okay? What is dispensationalism? Can I get a tattoo and does content matter? Should I store up food? Is it possible to be free of racial tension? How can I pray for this nation when there seems to be no hope? Why do my prayers go unanswered? Would it be okay to get in touch with my deceased family members? Could you see Heaven if you got close enough? Should my family become involved in Halloween and get a Christmas tree? Is there free will in Heaven? Are there gifts for the spirit today? I just want to end it all. What should I do? I mean, why? Will the Rapture happen this year? What is a Bar Mitzvah? Could a cloned human being be saved? Are powerful people secretly desperate? What is eternal life? If what matters is what's deep inside, how can I go to Heaven? Are names erased from the Book of Life? One time I had a dream about killing a black person. I'm not black. Does that mean I'm racist? How can I overcome health-related discouragement? What can I do to stop worrying? Do you have to be psychotic to make meaningful change in the world? And for a follow-up, is that what psychosis is for? Should we pluck out our eyes? I keep making mistakes. How can I stop? I mean, why? How do you plan to maintain this site after the Rapture? Do you have any fliers or pamphlets you could send me? Why won't you answer my e-mail? (http://www.raptureready.com/faq/rap23.html)

BLUFF

She chose, for the apocalypse, the Only Jeans That Truly Fit™. She stood on the bluff, on the highest of many mesas, one black boot raised on a boulder, leaning into her knee, squinting far beneath her sunglasses. The city looked like a cluster of crystals rising from the desert. In the background, her motorcycle pawed at the earth and revved its nostrils. From this vantage she watched the apocalypse coming, filling the desert with roiling black soot so fast it seemed always to have been there, gnarled, burled, paisley, churning, eddying, smoking, and soon the soot enveloped the city like a tsunami and surged around the mesas until all but her mesa were submerged, and the black clouds thrashed against the bluff and wallowed at her ankles. She felt her heart swell and then shrink beneath her tiny t-shirt. She turned on her heel to mount the steel steed, her body raw-er than ever and entirely less fleshy. She could see in the round silver ant-body-part part of the motorcycle how hard, how set, how hot, and how cold her face and eyes were now. She rode her motorcycle around the plateau. She began to take on the world by riding around the plateau feeling really powerful, gazing into the consistent distance until a trench formed beneath her tires. By the time she noticed, she couldn't hop the bike out. She dismounted and tried push it but her muscles must have been the kind you get at the gym that never work in real life. She longed for an actual steed, or to be an ant. And so she rode on, not knowing what else to do. Even now the trench walls rise.

VIEW

One of the difficult parts of the evening was standing in their birch-paneled great-room, windows over a cliff black with night. Besides the expense, the expanse, there was the man's penis from long ago, before he was married to this hostess in white.

She knew it curled in his herringbone trousers. The penis, keeper of her promiscuous past and container of the futures of many possible people.

It had been longer than usual.

It had been formative, lying near him and thinking about what an ass she was because he smelled to her like spoiled milk. The hostess had such strong brown arms.

It's difficult to think about futures without making a joke about money.

Above the long, smooth, knotty pine table (it's hard to think of knotty without the memory of deviant behavior; it's hard to think of pine without nostalgia) hung a painting of a woman as a landscape, like the very landscape visible from the great window it faced during the day, but not visible now, because it was night. It is possible the hostess painted it. Across a field of floor another couple lounged closely on a couch, the man so *in place* in this house, in his body, near this woman's bosom, that he was happily nodding off. The woman-as-landscape doesn't seem to be a painting of anyone; it seems to be a painting of the history of walking around on ladies. She viewed the painting as she'd viewed the room and the past before it.

Now she is on the other side of the glass with us, her feet over picturesque nothing. There are no current explosions. Someone's cooking in the kitchen. Someone's nodding on the couch. It's their house, it's their chasm, it's the view from their bodies.

REVIEW

These people in the photo of the war and their babies look like dirt and
rags in dirt. All fell, but especially the babies, who fell into the earth the
way they had always fallen into shoulders, into sleep, with small, complete
weight. You understand that the bodies are dead because of angles eluci-
dated by the photograph. You are not convinced that the stillness is not
the stillness of a photograph. As the photo suggests, you conflate what is
rag, what is dirt, what is body. You put yourself in there, even in babies,
and you know the angles your body can't do, even with yoga. The other
reason you know they're dead is it says as much on a little card next to
the photograph. You have come to an exhibit of photographs that has
been praised for breathing. The reviewer stopped short of announcing
that the pictures make the war come to life. He'd composed the review
after visiting an ex-lover in the hospital, a sculptor who "remained in
a vegetative state." In the hospital, he tried to concentrate on the sheet
veiling her and not the memory of her body. She had been a sculptor on
her way to revitalizing classicism. They lived in an apartment with her
resin figures. He had been a photographer losing faith in his own artistic promise. Her stillness was hard to take. He remembered the camera
he loved, a Nikon he'd saved up for in 1965 and still brought out sometimes, usually alone in his apartment, usually after several drinks. Once
he'd found a mysterious roll of film among the pieces of fruit in the bowl
on his countertop and had it developed. On it, objects in his life had been
rendered monumental. He had not had children. He had not gone to war.
He had not made good art, but when he looked at the photograph of his
kettle he found it difficult to breathe.

METAPHOR

At the brain stem, madness hunkered like a bomb the size of a baby's fist. It was not a stone, as our ancestors believed, because a stone remains stone. The bomb is scientific. Madness is mostly dis-integration. The little fist is a little baby's fist, but if the baby wiggles its fingers you're done for. Anything can happen to set the baby off. You can get raped, take drugs, or fall out with your mother. You can think a bad thought or a magic word. A baby can grow into all kinds of baby. You can go on with your life with the baby living in, off, or on your body. Madness is some of your eggs that you could ovulate now or never. Madness dams the river in your dick, hair over time in a drain. I know in the end it's not like you are one thing and madness is another. It is a sleeping fist of your own stone bomb dick dam babies.

VIRGINS

Never mind, this is what happened to Betsy. It's what they say. She grew a tail. They ripped it from her. It divided her butt. I'm kidding. But you know how you can tell when a girl loses her virginity is you look at her ass: if it's clenched up she's fine, but if it's got a space—like if you look at her ass you can tell because obviously there's room now—seriously, pay attention when you go by.

VERSIONS

Posters rose around the neighborhood describing a lost pigeon, which you might recognize because it might land on you. So meanwhile I've been hanging out with this very sexy girl Maggie who always wants to be with me but doesn't want to date me. She's recently lost-then-found her giant cat Hank, who's a typical tom that way. Then she went to Spain and people in her building were taking care of the cat, who is allowed to go in and out of the window. Back from Spain, there were posters around for another lost cat, and the owners called her house and tried to convince her that Hank was actually *their* cat, the new lost one. Maggie won by saying Hank was at least 30 percent bigger than their cat. I don't know if she knew their cat, or if it was an educated guess based on how big Hank truly is. "People appreciate data," she said to me. I was holding a towel in front of her so she could change at the lake. Naturally I'd been sort of trying to tamp down my crush and sort of trying to let it do what it wants. So then later that day when we got back from the lake and I dropped her off and was at my house getting ready to take myself to the movies, I heard scuffling on my roof and went outside to look. There was a giant white pigeon like a foot above me on my stoop's overhang thing, *huge* for a pigeon, with a pink beak and giant pink feet. It took off in a rush and a feather fell from it. I don't know what percent bigger. Then I went to the movies, not putting anything together. When I got home my land-ladies were sitting in the dark garden. I joined them for a nightcap and they told me about seeing this white bird in the yard. "I saw it too!" I said. That made me remember the poster for the pigeon. I felt worried that someone had been missing their tame bird all this time and I'd just gone to the movies, and I felt like I'd forgotten because I was getting all the posters mixed up with my stupid feelings for Maggie in some way. So the next day I walked all over the neighborhood until I found a poster, and then I called the number. It was a weird guy. There's a certain kind of weird guy in this town and they have a certain kind of voice, sort of lonely and sort of self-righteous. A kind of guy into ham radio. He said the poster was about a gray pigeon, not a white one with pink feet like the one I saw, but that he'd actually lost a white one, too, a while before that. He didn't sound at all freaked out, or relieved, or anything, and that started to make me mad.

Next day I was biking over to Maggie's and we were going to have brunch at a place that used to be a bank. There were leaves everywhere in the streets. I was thinking about the structure of many leaves coming from one tree. Then how they all fell away but there was still that one tree. I thought about money, about bicycling through money swirling around in the street surrounded by bald trees as if the money had come from the trees even though of course not. This is the way I use my brain. There in the street was a weird guy, and some distance away, maybe a house-worth of distance, there was a giant pigeon, and the guy was trying to coax it toward him. It was a black pigeon with red rims on its face. I didn't want to bicycle through them in this delicate moment so I pulled over. I watched the man and the pigeon move in relation to each other like backward magnets. A cat that looked a lot like Hank sat on a porch and was definitely watching, too. I tried to think of what percentage like Hank that cat was. Then I tried to think of what percentage like Hank the rest of us were, living on this Earth. No cars were coming. I realized there was no way the man would know I was the person who'd called him, if he was the man I'd called. So I said, "Hey! I've gotta get through here, okay?" I said it the way I've seen people with Hummers say that to people like construction workers, or anyone really. It's amazing how urgent something like brunch can feel. But the weird guy didn't look up from the pigeon. I could have just gone right ahead through them, but something made me not do that, even though the guy was on another planet. He was on another planet in some kind of system that was beyond me, something where he was in a network with a series of birds, white, gray, black, and maybe with a whole separate weird guy on the phone interacting in a series of patterns. They'd tacked up these flyers onto trees, and some of the flyers were crumbling onto the streets. I let the man keep staring at the bird and then I looked at the cat watching them, too, like me. I backed up and went around the block. When I got to Maggie's she was freaking out because she couldn't find Hank. She was afraid her neighbors might be harboring him. I said maybe he was just out chasing tail, and she threw a pillow at me. Then she went to make a phone call. I picked up the pillow and held it in front of me by two of its corners, the way I'd held up a towel a day ago. For a second I thought about the posters around town and let go of one of the corners. That's the opposite of a nail, if you think about it. Maggie and I are the same height, and we have basically the same haircut. We both wear glasses part-time and contacts part-time, but I really couldn't tell you if it's the same amounts. There could be so many more things to aim my feelings at, and sometimes I think the right thing is hovering just above my left ear. But it's like every time I move, whatever the right thing is moves in exact relation to me. It makes me really want to get out of here, this whole brainspace, this country, whatever made me the version of myself that I am.

PHONE

This boy on the phone on the porch across the courtyard in springtime lets his voice move, light as a leaf in a river: "It's like I'm only me when I'm around you." He's twirling a piece of grass between his thumb and forefinger, watching its head swivel. He's saying, "Don't tell anyone."

Dim through the walls behind him his friends are playing guitars with their amplifiers unplugged. They all have girlfriends somewhere, too. When the earth shakes and the dust of the world bounds across the lawn, when the posts that hold the porch roof snap, he feels no more misty and no less certain than he had the moment before. He says "I love you" into the phone and believes it exactly the same as he believed it before. The girl on the phone, who always feared he might not love her and never wondered if she loved him or not, feels the earth turning to powder as he says the words and thinks, *This must mean he really loves me*, and in the next instant thinks, *It doesn't count!* and by the next instant the end of the world has already happened. The telephone and an amplifier dot hillsides on opposite ends of the universe. The boy's eyelashes spin like a blown dandelion. The girl's fingernails sparkle in shards.

REAL ITALIANS

In all of the dreams it was an ornate bar and she had to walk by dozens of rich people, some of whom she knew to be his daughters by the way they looked like Sofia Coppola was going to look once everyone knew about her. They might leap up at any moment and kick her out for being a minor. When she'd get to him it was obvious that his Cadillac lay, like a chocolate bar, in the street outside, with its same car phone hanging up between the front seats and its cord, like all the phones' cords back then, dreamily flopping between the seats, him calling from it, still not impressing her, even as she left the bar full of his daughters and got into it all over again.

But in the bar, where they never were in real life, she remembers talking about the apocalypse: he asked her what she'd wear, "What would you wear the last night on earth?" and she said, "I don't have anything good," and he starts listing clothes he likes. She can't tell if he thinks she has these clothes, or if he's just listing ideas, but every outfit he says she can see hanging, ready for anything. What's important is how one person's fantasies can start taking over another's.

He keeps talking about his plans with Robert De Niro, who he heard is looking for real Italians. She keeps trying to remember an obvious song by Blondie. He did turn out to be a minor henchman in a bunch of shows since then. She got a clip from one where he gets offed by getting shot and falling from a pier into the water. She put it where she can click it on her desktop, so in some dreams he falls back over and over with his hand reaching for that brass rail and she's yelling at him: "But you're only a minor dealer! I'm the one with the future!" She does remember when she first saw him on TV, though, and what's killing her—and this might be what connects the forms the dreams about him take—is that she really was impressed, as if he'd made it.

VIBRISSAE

I loved her, but the day before the storm she kept coming into my room and looking at me. She knows what gets on my nerves. That, along with her cats, my dog, everyone. The plants down the street, the bundles of garbage that float by our windows and roll along the sidewalks, snow-balling like human souls. This is why we lived twitching, as if we'd ever sense what could help us.

GHOSTS

She draws her bath, blue with salts, and from the bedroom, we, the ghost of everyone who loved her, feel its terrible fumes. We watch, squirming among the folds of the comforter, ghost like smoke, like the coils of a brain, like fleshy roots pale from never having seen sun, massed and white—ghosts are always pale, significantly *blanched*. She covers her limbs with soap; she stands to do it, lathering every port and gulley. How can she rinse in such blue water? And then how can it be so invisible against her skin when the smells roll under the door and surf the hallway? When she comes out and it's clear from her face that she knows we're here, she challenges us, with her silence, to say something. But we have no mouths and she knows it, so what sort of challenge is that? She's wearing nothing but her towel turban. She's pale and strong, but not yet dead. Her eyelashes are dark because they're still wet. She puts her palm flat on her dressing table and leans hard, toward the mirror. We have no weight, and we are afraid of mirrors, which are our equals in transparency. This mirror is oval and swivels on mahogany pegs, as all good mirrors should. She drinks from a small glass of scotch and doesn't bother about the ring it leaves. It's not our business anymore, what she does to the furniture. We want to shoot her. Sure, with a gun, shoot her full of holes so blue salty worms can crawl in and consume her from the inside out. She takes a tiny brush from a tiny drawer and uses it on her eyebrows. We scurry around her ankles, catching the last of the wet heat. Then there's no more wet heat, only some droplets jiggling on her calves. We squirm and wait for the clothes to come out. Then they do. We want to pounce but we wait through all the possible outfits, and finally of all t-shirts and jeans she has chosen the right ones.

We cling best to cotton. We grin with our whole body. She'll feel wisps of us all night, fingers in her ears, peripheral ticks in the atmosphere. But sooner or later she'll strip, and there'll be nothing we can do but hunch in a wad in the corner as she coils around this new person who fucks and fucks, making the sounds of life. But we don't stop grinning yet.

SESAME

Two lovers stood at the door to Aladdin's cave. They'd been at it forever. They each believed they were still in love, if only they could think of the right thing to say. They remembered magic words from childhood. But this was an apocalypse, so no such luck. They stood at the door to the cave, admiring a door that fits a cave. One of them thought about man and nature. One of them took her clothes off and struck a pose, shivering. An old lady came hobbling along in a cloak with a basket and offered them a million dollars from it if they'd do it right there in front of her. They did it and she gave them the million dollars, and they pushed it through the mail slot but the door still didn't open. They were going to run their fingers through heaps of coins and put golden vessels over their heads like helmets, for fun. They wouldn't come out of the cave, and they wouldn't let anyone in, either, no matter what anyone said or what was shoved through the mail slot. Then another old lady came along in a cloak with a basket. "What's in your basket?" they asked. The old woman said "Bread," and suddenly the lovers were so hungry they offered to do it right there in front of her if she'd give them the bread, but the woman just rolled her eyes and hobbled off, muttering about the arrogance of young people.

AIRPORT HILTON

In the front lobby in the middle of everything was a choice of two restaurants: Buddy's or Chang's.

In my room, number thirty thousand and something, I turned off the television because I heard a violin. The whole point of a violin is to kill you emotionally. I listened, and then I slipped into the pink and yellow hall and followed its glowing geometry. The communal jetlag of so many unseen people puffed weakly from under doors like in Batman when someone floods a room with poison-gas.

The violin made me, in the hotel, odd, beautiful, alien, and heart-filled. The violin was practicing, and it had no irony, a beyond-world-class violin, finer than the Met or whatever you like, stopping and starting anywhere in any number of pieces. The violin in the pieces was like me in the hotel. The hotel was as pink, yellow, and winding as intestines, as my own shining unspilled guts.

I like the test at the eye doctor's where you put your head in a white globe with a cross made of black pinholes and press a button with your thumb when you see a white light in your peripheral vision. After a few minutes your thumb joins the automatic systems of your body, communicating with the light on its own.

A game I play with lovers who let me is I close my eyes and then I like them to touch me with one finger here and then there, just so I don't know some things, but not so I don't know anything. Like any reasonable apocalypse, pulsing with intimacy and the anonymous. I like the long hall of doors and the garish light and my ear near the cool wall covering. Any moment any door might open and any person might appear in front of a bed around any corner, my heart beating as it beat when I was a child hidden for hide and seek, although here I am exposed and still secret, just like naked. I slide to the carpet in the hall because I want to be stiller than I can be teetering on two feet, and

I kneel on the way to prostration with my ear to the wall in the face of danger.

HIDE AND SEEK

Dark
Hidden
People searching
Among children I am afraid don't love me
Sound of children: pretty annoying
Round shape of hilly neighborhood
Not doing anything wrong
Fantasy of: quick terror of being found; slow realistic agony of not being found, this being what? Winning? Because on this planet the goal is to be alone forever? But instead of everyone calling "You win! Come out! We can't bear it without you!" they forget what they were looking for & roast marshmallows on a hundred sticks.

HALLWAY WITH VIOLIN

Pink & Yellow
Exposed
Accidental "discovery" possible
Anonymous
Violin: my favorite
Elbow angles of hotel in space
Eavesdropping &/or masturbating
Fantasy of: asking the concierge to pass my secret message to the violinist. We agree via knowing looks that a famous violinist is in the hotel but we say aloud, in the language we share but which is foreign to both of us, that it must be a very talented amateur no one in the hotel would want to ambush. Then the violinist crosses to my room in the night in a black gown. She is Chinese because I dug tunnels there throughout childhood, & I am still me. She is melancholic. Suddenly she explains some of the things she has to say via the violin, which everyone knows is the body. We drink something fizzy that will almost kill you but only almost, & watch some television, lying on the bed on our stomachs like twins but I'm blonde. I never know what I'm wearing. I'm usually invisible. I'm my eyes & voice, my elbows on the bedspread, my hands circling my glass like they've come to life around the waist of a doll. We turn off the television. The space that surrounds the hotel swoops into the room. The room is filled with stars. The stars are the jetlagged people of the world shoved beyond orbit. Everything is inside-out, we've turned the corner at the far end of the Big Bang, I mean the hotel, I mean the tunnels through my brain, I mean my body, I guess it has to be my body, & we are returning to the center of everything, with the best view, not to mention the soundtrack I always wanted to tell me how to feel & what to do.

ADOGALYPSE

After the apocalypse, she missed her dog. One thing she thought about the apocalypse was you're supposed to have a dog. She'd take a zombie dog, if only so she'd get to kill it cathartically and as a symbol of all she'd lost, including her real dog who died a week before the apocalypse in the backseat of her car while they were driving to the vet. She heard his organs contract and then release forever. She heard his death rattle, the only one she'd ever heard, then and now, because the apocalypse was a loud one and you'd think you'd hear death rattles like echoes for days but the boom lasted long enough that when it stopped all she heard was the memory of her own dog's natural death. She wasn't able to pull over. It was night, the road was twisty, and she was not letting herself believe this was it. She'd kept driving, telling him it was okay. "Okay, baby. Good boy. It's gonna be okay." Now she knew from experience, because here on the other side of the apocalypse she was supposedly okay, too.

COUCH

I take my brother to his psychiatrist. We were up late, don't ask. We're pretty fried. Waiting room has a couch, two cushy armchairs, a coffee table, end tables with magazines, and a few toys for kids. It appears both abandoned and armed. No one there but a receptionist behind glass.

My brother goes in. I lie on the couch.

He's in there with his psychiatrist. He's talking about his problems, some probably involve me. I go into a grateful doze.

Lady comes out from behind glass and says, "Will you sit up, please?" I can hear in her voice that it's been building.

Is it my feet? My feet are not on the couch, I was careful about that. She says, "You're disturbing clients."

"No one's here," I say.

She says there won't be room when they come.

"I'll get up if they come," I say, but there's no use, I've already lost. I pick out one thing from many options relating to her appearance to scoff at silently. I draw a parallel between two kinds of one-sided conversations. Then I think of a couple more. I picture my brother in the next room trying to come up with the truth. I picture all the people in our lives piling up in the room with him and his psychiatrist. People with real problems. If I said one more thing the lady would invoke policy. So I sit up. Do we feel better now?

MATH

I was talking, at a party, with a man about *Lolita*. He seemed surprised that we both liked it. I told him it was a very well-liked book. He was being really flirty. First when we met at the party he just looked at me, and then as soon as I said something he said, "You're witty!" He reminded me of someone and I was trying to think of who it was. I figured out that he looked like a friend of mine—a writer who's written a book about *Lolita*, and also some novels. I told him. Now he said, "Is your friend a good writer?" Well, he's well liked.

I thought of this other writer I know, who looks like a famous actor—everyone says so, and he's even written about it. He was the teacher of another writer friend of mine. I was at her place the other day and met her ex-husband, and you know who he looks like? That famous actor, and consequently also that writer who looks like him, my friend's teacher. I mentioned this to them and neither one had ever noticed that he looked like anyone, but they agreed completely, so I'm not making it up.

In light of all this, it's interesting to me that when we read a book we don't look like anyone. And also, something I thought about during both *Lolita* movies: how important it is, in the book, that we don't see her except in our imagination, because if we saw her she'd be just a kid and we'd freak out. I thought about that music video with sexy Liv Tyler and her father lusting over her as if we don't know he's her father. But maybe the goal is we *do* know he's her father. So what about the guy at the party? God, I hardly remember him, except he was a math genius. But I remember hoping all the time we were talking that he could quickly explain math to me, suddenly, in an ejaculate burst, in a way that I'd really get it, all the parts of math that I always longed for, that I knew were on the other side of all the math I couldn't bear, and because of this I have the same lingering sense of loss that I might have had if we'd slept together, or been married once for several years, a long time ago.

DINOSAUR

A dinosaur lay under a rainbow in a white sunset on shining hills. The girl, a sample girl, a remnant, reached for the imaginary hand of the ghost. The ghost had been trailing her across state after state, holding his basket, ever since the apocalypse. In the basket, tiny ghosts of prairie dogs and butterflies, mongeese and baby foxes, wobbled, nested, nuzzling in their contained afterlife. The vast exposed land, its lid lifted, its whole history layered under the grass, now history—girl, dinosaur, ghost, basket—teetering on the deserted road in the light air. The dinosaur's anchor-shaped nose brushed the grass tips at its knees. Plateaus of clouds seemed still. The hand of the ghost was not a hand, it was the memory of hands, or now, since the apocalypse, the idea that a hand could come. She missed a horse she'd known as a child. Purple flowers massed and then spread thinly over the field. Yellow flowers made a wave near the road. She remembered how many people must have used to have been about to awaken each moment. With so little left after the silent blast that razed so much and left so much as well—too much to take in, to count, witness, know, hunt, cover, recall—she didn't know what to do with her still-empty hand full as it was to be, if she could reach it, with that much ghost. The dinosaur looked heavy, the rainbow looked light, and the hills could have been covered in snow, or nothing, or something that had never existed before.

II.
UP TO HALF THE
APOCALYPSES

numbed out from the past

MEMORY

When I was a boy and they told us to lie down on the San Andreas Fault to feel the tremors, I didn't feel anything. Reminds me: not long before that I was in *The Pied Piper*, cast as a witch who had one early scene and one late scene. In the first scene, the Pied Piper said a line from the last scene, so I pictured the line in the script, white next to mine in yellow highlighter, and as I pronounced the line that followed it—my line, what I was meant to say, as I saw it—all the rats' eyes went shifty. But everyone proceeded directly to the end of the play from there, and even the kids who never made it to the stage took their curtain call responsibly. At home, times like these, my mother would always say, "You're being so sensitive, it's not the end of the world," and I thought, *Well then what is the end of the world?* I never found out from her, so I imagined the apocalypse. I thought about how weird it would be to be a horse and have a crop hit you behind the saddle out of nowhere.

NOSTALGIA

We were so close from five to eight. We had one last fight and I hung up knowing it was the end, feeling bittersweet for what I would later know was the first time, remembering how future nostalgia thickened the hallway surrounding the telephone, all the familiar furniture taking one step from the walls into the carpet, as if I could see each piece through the plaster.

Soon we moved away and then at twenty I made a detour back through town. In the fields, kids I'd been five with were coaches. I ate a nostalgic pastrami sandwich. I drove by her house and there she was, like magic, mowing her parents' lawn. In the kitchen we drank tea out of a brown pot I hadn't known I'd forgotten, and the squeak when I pulled in my chair felt so familiar it was like nothing I'd felt before. When we were kids she'd been very nearly blind, with big glasses and googly eyes. Now she was hot. I said, "Where's your glasses?" She said she only pretended to wear contacts in high school and taught herself to see. Later I asked this current blind friend of mine about that and she said it sounded like bullshit. She said I only believed her because I thought she was so hot. She said I was full of shit, verging on fetishistic.

After the apocalypse I was wandering around thinking about real magic. Leaves of newspapers still cart wheeled along the streets sometimes, but I'd stopped reading them. I'd given in to the process of forgetting, of letting the past go, of letting it rise from the depths of reflective surfaces on its own, all of this as if the world, eradicated, had a will. Back with the teapot, I'd looked into her eyes and known she'd told the truth. But now I think the eyes aren't the windows to anything. Instead I hold on to the idea that the past is the past for some reason.

DOUBLE NOSTALGIA

One of the problems of pre-school-aged children is that of communication. The vocabulary of such children is limited and variable. The child may call a bird a chicken, or a jeep a car, etc. Thus, the examiner must discriminate between the child who cannot see and the child who offers an unexpected word for what he sees. In youth, the focusing lenses of the eyes are very elastic; most children can focus objects even three inches from their nose. As we grow older, the focusing lenses gradually lose their elasticity and at 35 to 38 years of age, difficulty is experienced in increasing lens curvatures to enable us to focus on objects that are near; this condition is called PRESBYOPIA. There are six muscles attached to the outside of each eyeball to accomplish turning the eyes. The supply of nervous energy to these muscles determines the balance, or parallelism, of the visual axes. Worth noting is the importance of having multiple eyes, which must be manipulated, by the brain, time, technology, or other therapies, in order to function in concert. If a person can maintain balance, HETEROPHORIA exists. If imbalance becomes manifest, HETEROTROPIA exists.

M	VISION TEST CARD	POINT TYPE

.50 The airplane moved at a huge number of mph and in her seat it felt relatively motionless. Between motion and stillness are vibrations. Her fingers tittered along the grid of buttons on her tiny computer. When the man across the aisle looked at her hand moving, even though he also had a computer, and they worked in the same language, and they were both trained typists, he couldn't tell from watching her fingers what she was writing. Maybe if he'd been a lip reader. All the codes were the same, and still, the aisle was only this side of infinite. Maybe if he'd been a mind reader. These two were meant for each other. Her fingers moved like marionettes, with invisible strings into the ceiling. His did, too. They each had their own puppeteer hunched near the thick ceiling, chatting together, in their own world. What else? **4**

.63 The plane moved around the world and the world moved too, but, to the plane, seemed still. His mind moved to memories of watching video depictions of the solar system and he placed himself as a stick figure on Jupiter within the machine. When the plane lurched and hovered for a moment in an air pocket, he mistook the moment for imagining his stick-figure self experiencing an animated demonstration of centrifugal force. Across the aisle the eyes of the woman zigzagged like cartoon wariness, following the motion of the accumulating text he couldn't see, which in her mind moved forward only, one word after another, but on her screen moved like methodical paint filling in a wall, and what else: **5**

.80 She was writing about imaginary people moving within houses on a planet. A boy in her head moved a plastic airplane through the water in his bathtub, the airplane's windows almost completely rubbed away from use, action, friction, motion. The people in the writing moved according to the laws of physics as she'd learned them. They moved, she hoped, truthfully. Then she paused, taking a conscious breath. In her mind was a remembered idea of the future (think Jetsons but personal, and probably something about handsome/wedding from when she was six). She wriggled her hand into her lap under the tray table and adjusted the pinching seatbelt buckle. As if nudged, she looked across the aisle, but the man was facing his computer. Because of her angle, she couldn't see his eyes moving. He was reading or he was looking. If you looked at their eyes from the aisle, if you could take in so many eyes at once while following their gazes (which you couldn't), then you could see, if your rhythm was right, in a chance of one in just-this-side-of-impossible, their eyes do a bounce across the aisle: **6.3**

1.25 She'd look at her computer and then look at him three times, and he'd do the same to her but in reverse, and not only that but the kicker is they were thinking exactly the same thing (about ponies) and they were meaning exactly the same thing by it (secret of the universe); if you were fantastic and mathematical, and if you were the space between them, in front of them and slightly above them and a little inside them, then you could see with whatever your eyes would be in that situation that this really happened, seriously, no joke. But you will have to take my word for it. I'm so sorry, because it was so tragic and beautiful, not to be missed. Tragedy, tragedy, everything is like this, there's never anything else. It's a goddamn miracle that I live to tell. **10**

The adjustment of the Project-O-Chart for proper character size should be made in the usual manner as indicated in P.O.C. instruction manual using the 20/200 "E."

BABY ALIVE

(2012) 109 MINUTES

Detective Wendy Buckem (Sissy Spacek) finds herself on the trail of a killer targeting young mothers-to-be. Part thriller, part reality TV, the cast features MTV *Teen Mom* and *16 and Pregnant* reality stars (Catelynn, Farrah, Amber, Maci, Leah, Emily, Ebony, and Whitney). The young women struggle with their relationships, dreams, and new responsibilities while attempting to evade a mysterious stalker. As time runs out and bodies pile up, Detective Buckem finds herself confronting her own past. Also starring John Stamos.

REVIEWS

★★★★★

Baby Alive sucks you in and never lets you go. If you want action with raw emotion and the added bonus of REAL people that lends an air of ambiguity this movie will intrigue and inspire.

★★★★

I saw this movie in pre-release and found disjointed the attempt to merge so-called "reality" with actual celebrity within the same medium. Still, the plot itself is both familiar and functional, structured as a series of vignettes (or "episodes") in which we meet each teen mother before, during, or after her pregnancy, such that, prior to each grisly demise, earlier mothers are making the decision to have unprotected sex with their boyfriends (or sometimes acquaintances or assailants), and later scenes show the young ladies increasingly pregnant, and so on. Thereby an interesting effect occurs with respect to time, which I could get into further though not in this format. Some of the most affecting portrayals are actually the minor characters—the teen's family members, friends, and so on—who subtly look askance at the proceedings, and are in various ways positioned by force or happenstance to observe, as well, the killings, but then disappear from the film, not to get too deep, but perhaps like life itself? In any case, the actors who play these minor characters are sometimes diamonds in the rough. Overall, the film merits a 3.5, but as that option is not available I give it 4 with the benefit of the doubt.

★★★★★

The movie, enjoyable as it was, left me with many lingering questions. It doesn't say what he wants with the babies, even though there are only a few just near the end. I know that some of the fathers we're suppose to think are good father figures so maybe the babies left over go with him but maybe there's a sequel about the real dads? I found that aspect confusing. Otherwise this movie is good, and I was engaged as to the internal lives at hand. I know characters curse a lot in real life, but I also feel that you didn't need to have that many curse words to make your point.

★★★★★

Go Catelynn! I knew her in high school and she was never all that but you gotta respect she made more of her life than I did ha!

★★★

How did they get Sissy Spacek to do this movie? Sissy Spacek of *Coal Miner's Daughter* and *Carrie* and *Badlands*!? She is a class act, she must be having money problems? I saw her last year at a farmer's market in Virginia buying a bottle of olive oil for like twenty bucks so I don't get it at all. I liked the movie though, it was worth the price of a ticket.

★★★★

I am very selective when it comes to giving a five-star rating but this movie was awesome and it would have got five stars except for there was a little repetition in the methods the killer used—I know serial killers have to do it the same way because they are compelled, but I also feel like swords are a little overdone and the director could of mixed it up a bit more. Other than that it was fantastic viewing. John Stamos as the son/villain lends an air of brooding sophistication to the young cast.

★

This movie arrived cracked and when you kindly replaced it with another one I was unable to turn off the dubbing which was Chinese or something, making for an infuriating experience. You should have a way to rate it zero stars.

★★★★

Besides being a genuine suspenseful this film has many Themes and issues that it portrays. I enjoyed the symbol of the pacifier, or "nubbin" as it pertained to the serial killing/cutting body parts off aspect of the film. In terms of society at large, many of us have felt this way, and it lends a sense of reality to the relatable nature within the main character. There are some good comebacks in it and surprise twists. When I go to the movies I don't need it to be Academy Award Worthy however you should at least know how to act so I have to admit some of the teen moms did seem scared. I was also appreciative of the production value, which is one thing that always kept me from enjoying the television version and Reality TV in general.

★★★

Perhaps this movie was meant to be a satire, but someone in marketing didn't think that would sell? I heard that the original trailer featured the classic song "Baby's Got Back" which is hysterical, but someone nixed it or got offended which is why they switched to serious.

★

I had that doll as a kid and was expecting a movie inspired by it, but if that's the case for you, you will be surely disappointed in this travesty of a film production. What we really want is to be entertained, instead you get something totally unexpected. You may remember Baby Alive as big compared to the usual dolls and pretty realistic. It came with a baby food assemblage and poop. You know Transformers is from toys right? I bet half of you don't even know, you just want to bang Megan Fox who doesn't. It's one thing for an artist to be inspired but it's another thing to rip something off and not even know it. I know it's geeky but I got a lot of education about life from that doll.

★★★★★

This film seems like it's all about the gore of the killer, but in the end it does have an uplifting message about the value of each and every child. I'm not saying it's the greatest movie ever, but I and my date both enjoyed it.

★★★

I am a teen mom and my own mother was murdered when my child was two months old. I'm sorry if that is TMI but only recently have I decided to try to watch movies because it's hard to find one that isn't triggering. So I think people should consider that. I saw this movie in the theater which was the first time I had been in a movie theater in I don't know how long. It was in a falling apart old-school one downtown that is practically out of business but keeps hanging on. I don't remember much about the movie all I can say is I was glad I went, it was a big step for me in my life. Maybe someday I will be desensitized enough for a fuller appreciation.

★★★★

First off this movie is not about the Baby Alive doll, it's about twelve reality star teen moms that SPOILER ALERT get knocked off one by one in the grand tradition of this type of movie, where the black guy either died first or by the end of the 80s he died second to last by saving everyone by selfless sacrificing his life, underlining a mirror of racism. The moms are actually pretty inspiring when you consider how hard it is to raise a baby in this day and age. I kind of knew about halfway who the killer is, but I've seen a lot of movies like this and usually I know by the end of the credits so that's pretty good. There is also, for your information, a mechanical french duck from steampunk times that I saw in a museum that does the same thing as the doll with digesting etc. There's also a poem.

★★★★★

I remember that doll my friend had it! Gross! Also the teen moms need to get a life! But now they're dead!

RECALL

Not long after the mad cows they started recalling pistachios. Pistachios: the green flesh and flaking shells of our youth. So many things had been recalled. Hybrid production accelerated until even hybrids are being recalled. People gathered in fields to remember the food that fed them and killed them. They sang of the salads, the fruits, and the meats.

WITCHES

Three girls, maybe eight each, lean over a pothole of water, stirring with sticks. It's hard to tell, because they're frozen, although it's summer. They're looking into the water together, with their sticks. Dim oils sketch the surface like lines from skating. One girl, the one in the middle, from this angle anyway, has a piece of grass between her teeth, and she's grimacing. The end of the blade has fluffy seeds, and normally it'd be bobbing in the breeze. In this apocalypse, the air, it seems, can move, though nothing in it can. Where do you draw the line? Even seeds that could drift like smoke stick, no logic in it. Especially with pages accumulating, time continuing to pass. The girl on the supposed left is turning to dust as we speak, but invisibly, like a figure made of icing going stale, touch her and *poof*.

I know what they were doing. The girls were playing "three witches." They were making magic. They were poking their stew. They kept meaning to get on with their game. They'd planned to capture someone, and they'd planned to turn a bunch of things into other things. But after a while the entire plot had been taken over by recipes for potions.

ORPHAN IN THE CARDS

It's the future, in the morning sun, and there are more orphans than ever. A plane crashed in the background, in October. Spiderwebs covered the field in a sheen like water, sparks like the jewels of yore.

At the edge of the field she felt like a bell in her coat. The shadows of a flock of birds spun on the ground like a blizzard. The shadow of the flock of birds moved from the shape of a spade to the shape of a club. She'd always felt great at a buffet, and a buffet is like history because you can pick. She remembered her mother, the way she'd look up. She remembered her father, like spilled milk. She might have chosen another card. She might have picked up on another song. "What's that beautiful song?" she'd asked eons ago, and it was arpeggios, the stuff of life.

She was about to live out the rest of her days. She was looking into all three options, eyes in her head, eyes in the back of her head, two eyes that beat as one.

BABIES

They were cute, but they didn't know anything. They were full of shit babies and they kept her, when she came home from the shit in her life, from recovering, from what do you call it—healing, from learning. They didn't know anything but they were busy, they were drawing pictures and developing their sensibilities. They were cute, and they were fun, too, they thought of such *original* things, and they helped her, they made her forget—wait, no, not forgetting, but feeling like she was making something, making something out of *babies*, even though they had no idea, they were mostly drawing pictures and coming up with shit. She thought she could keep them clean. She thought she could keep the shit outside, she thought she could take it outside, she thought she could leave it outside, but when they grew older so much shit would happen to them, as it had happened to her—they would get beat, shit would rain from the sky on them, too, what do you say about weathering vs. weathering a storm, a shitstorm. Well, in the future they weathered it, in the future she went back into the house, they were gone, she flew around in there, in the house with everything her kids made that held up the walls.

MIRACLES

We watched our father take the jar out to the patio on the day we had been waiting for ever since he put the spider into it with its egg sac. It was a black widow spider which we knew never to touch in the garden and to know by the red bow on its belly. We'd been living in the country since our stark raving mad mother started calling the apartment from her orbit. Our father lay down near the jar, on his side. He was always showing us stuff around the farm. He was growing a beard, always tired and patient. There was a barn with a horse in it we were taking care of. He said a lot about learning to take care of others as a part of growing up, and we watched him with eyes too big for our heads. We gathered around the jar and put our noses to it in turn, looking for the movement he said to look for in the egg sac, how you could see it was time by shadows crossing. We were getting a little bored when the babies started to come out, just like he said. They were smaller than anything, and the big mother spider, you couldn't tell if she was paying attention. The babies were spreading out over the inside of the jar, the miracle of life. They were making their ways to the air holes punched in the lid. Our father just watched and commented for our benefit. He put a stick to an air hole and we watched babies crawl up it. Spiders crawl their whole lives. We watched, but some of our attention wandered. We were new to the countryside, new life surrounding us. I remember a lot of things from that place besides this. After the apocalypse, a brother of mine said, "Do you remember if you were nervous with all those poison spiders radiating from the jar? Do you remember that we didn't have any insect spray because we'd just moved out there but he had a can of hairspray and that's what he sprayed on them, just as they were getting away? Why did we have hairspray? Was it hers?"

TIME MACHINE

He arrived at her house on his bicycle, chained it to her porch, buckled his helmet to the rear rack, and knocked. A helmet, seriously, now he has a helmet and it's not for hockey, not for a Ducati, it's for a *bicycle*. He hadn't wanted to drive, because he was afraid he might run over something.

She opened the door, wearing, at four in the afternoon, men's flannel pajamas rolled to the knees and elbows, her hair held back with a pencil, a second pencil behind her ear, and a third pencil in the pocket of the flannel top. "You," she said, and tilted her head, which made the pencil behind the ear slip, which she caught and held in her teeth like a rose. Instantly he liked her house. He stood in the doorway, then stepped in as she stepped away and they both stood in the half-moon foyer. He tried to think of why he liked the house, and it was the smell. It didn't smell like his house, he realized; what his house smelled like was baby, because of the baby. They had a flirty thing at work. At work she'd said, "Come over, I'll show you my sketches." But here she was with the pencils. She wasn't an artist; by her own account, she was a closet writer. Still he held out hope.

"Thank you for this," he said in the blank space that made up the entrance. Nothing had even happened yet and he really meant it, because of the hope.

She helped him take off his windbreaker and left to put it somewhere. He looked around the living room and then sat on the sofa. Everything was so harmless. He went to her fridge and got a soda. Harmless, rooting around her fridge. He sat back on the sofa, pushing a blanket into a lump on the other side. Harmless. She'd come over and pick up the blanket and sit where it had been and lean against the arm of the sofa with her knees up and her feet pointing at him. They'd be like two machine parts at angles on velvet outside of time. The soda was harsh and he remembered wondering as a kid how they could call it a soft drink. *I'll have a soft drink*, he imagined saying with tiny "ha-ha-ha" huffs from a scene like this. What's so funny? A scene from the '50s in which next she'd appear in something *more* comfortable than men's pajamas. What happened was he felt self-conscious. Instantly, hope was gone.

That's when he saw it: as if in place of hope was a structure the size of a voting booth or a Porta Potty, over near the fireplace. The structure was composed of heavy-duty plastic, cylindrical, size Adult, in midnight blue, with blue curtains. He put his soda down on the glass top of the coffee table and approached the structure cautiously. He poked the curtain. "What're you doing?" he called, but the curtain sucked up his voice.

He drew the curtain and stepped inside. He drew the curtain again and stood in darkness.

The booth, if anyone asked him, he would have to say, in all earnestness, recognized him. In the dark he cycled through his senses: he felt fizzy, as if he'd been lowered into a giant body-temp version of what he'd been drinking. The lack of the smell of baby was overwhelming, mingled with the lack of the scent of his marriage, and then to top it off the lack of the scent of a woman with pencils in her hair. The inside of his mouth was still sweet. He heard faint static, and then he realized the booth was mic'd. Little colored lights were waking up all around him, even under his feet. The mic spat and then he heard the woman say through the speaker, as if shockingly near and calling anyway, "In a minute, I'm writing something down before I forget." In the booth, more and more lights were blinking on and establishing independent rhythms. He could sort of see by them, but all there was to see were the blinking lights, the patterns of blinks and buttons in red, green, and white. *It does know me*, he thought. The booth began to shake a little. He didn't know what to do. He could hop out or he could blast off, or something else that he couldn't think of. He was so scared he took his penis out and started fooling around with it. He kept his eyes open to the cacophony of tiny lights. He hoped beyond hope that by the time he was done he'd know, by god, what would happen next.

APOCALYPSES PAST

After the apocalypse we didn't even talk about all the crap we'd read about it before or seen in movies. Like we were embarrassed of our whole species' imagination. Even what we'd gotten right just seemed lame and obvious. It was a new taboo, talking about the predictions, uncool to do, as opposed to cannibalism, which was pretty reasonable, or wanton sex, which was necessary, heroic even, given the state of so many of our physiques. One night or day or whatever it was, we were sitting around a campfire and I was like, *What do I keep trying to remember?* And it was ghost stories. I mean never in real life did I ever actually tell a ghost story. I just saw it in so many movies it seemed like, having been a kid, I must have done it. Like stealing cookies from a jar, which I never did either. Who has a cookie jar? No one ever again, you can bet on it! So there we were, all fucking and eating each other by the fire, and I kept having all these apocalypse stories from my childhood right there on the tip of my tongue, but for everyone's sake, I held back.

TIME CAPSULES

Forty years later, a bunch of us noticed that our elementary schools had never contacted us about digging up those time capsules. At first we saw this as another reason to have lost faith in our bodies and our homes. Then, as we wiped the sperm from each other and climbed from the wreckage of our Mini Coopers and settled into life in our yurts, we thought maybe the lesson was that no one's keeping track except you. We thought, *Maybe in our golden years.* We thought, *Maybe next life.* Many of our elementary schools are gone, many are converted, many are 100 percent remodeled, from carpet to duct, and repopulated kid by teacher by custodial staff. Mostly only latitude and longitude is the same, and sometimes the name, usually of a person no one remembers. Our bodies have replaced all of our cells several times over, something we tripped out on together in our twenties, and still, we are what we are. Nothing is the same outside the body, and you are putting your body into stuff that is not you all day and all night with the force of your will, more and more the more you age, beaming onto the world like headlights from outer space or another epoch.

ZOMBIES

Last town, he'd lived near the tracks, heard the train, and no one did anything to prepare for Halloween. Some raided the fridge for eggs, evidently. Halloween was like most days, fear in the air. It marked time in the nation, in a parade with the other holidays. One year in that town he made a rule for the neighborhood kids: no costumes, no candy. He got together a bag of rags, masking tape, and markers from around the house. When kids arrived in jeans and t-shirts he wrapped one kid in shredded sheets: "Look, you're a mummy, here's your candy"; and he wrapped another one in shredded sheets: "Look you're a Vietnam Vet, back from the dead."

"I'm a mummy!" kids cried. "I'm back from the dead!"

But here, the kids across the cul-de-sac had lined their porch with intricate pumpkins. He went over to look at them. "That one's bored, that one's perplexed, that one's ambivalent," the boy said, pointing with a knife much too big and sharp for his body, but suited to his pirate outfit. The older sister, a girl in the tenth grade who practiced piano every evening, had used a pattern from a magazine to carve a wolf howling at the moon, with more and less pumpkin carved out to create depth, character, and shadow. She was inside the house, practicing. She was just about as close to him as the boy, but veiled through the window screen.

"You've got some complex pumpkins over here," he said to the boy.

"That's not complex," said the boy. "That doesn't even *begin* to be complex."

In this town he lived near the tracks, too, but on the other side, the construction of a new development paused indefinitely, a dozen houses wrapped in Tyvek.

He fixed a drink and took a chair to his porch and sat with his basket of assorted miniatures. He liked Halloween. He liked the dying and then undying. When he was a kid he said he wanted to be a boat and his aunt made him a boat to wear. He was the captain and he was also the boat, the aunt explained. His parents and their friends gathered around him in their witches' hats, with bright cocktails, and complimented him. But he still felt like he was just the captain, walking around in a boat.

This town was a lot like the town he'd grown up in, something he'd been working toward for a long time. It had been a hard bunch of years. *I'm back from the dead*, he'd thought, dropping the last box into his new living room. Here, though, the kids eyed him just as suspiciously. They eyed him with better vocabularies. And here, he felt himself looking at the town with as much bewilderment as he'd looked at the adults in the town where he'd been a child. Only now he was an adult. He walked with his drink to the center of the cul-de-sac. He turned around and around, just enough to get a little dizzy. Then he tried to aim himself home.

But the apocalypse is not the wobbling away. The wobbling away is life persisting. The apocalypse is him spinning, with the drink *clink-clink-ing*, delicate potential to go faster and faster, to drill a hole into the earth with his body—or—and—alternately, to dissipate centrifugally like rings through water, into droplets, into air.

STAR CHART

We took a day trip to San Francisco and I wanted dim sum which I've never gotten to eat but my uncle basically ordered only shrimp and one pork thing and the pork thing was so divine, I just haven't had anything like it—it was so cinnamony and had puffy white bun stuff around it. Like a cake you might make. But all the rest was one delicious yet almost identical shrimp thing after another. My uncle sensed from us girls a bit of boredom with the shrimp. He said, "I just wanted to show you what I like."

He's a glassblower and he makes a lot of fish to sell. He also scuba dives and goes on fly-fishing trips and deep-sea fishing trips. He also collects fish figures, especially realistic ones. One time when I was visiting he was swimming and got stung by a whole mass of jellyfish and came back to the house covered in whip marks, but he was so quiet and just sat there while my aunt put meat tenderizer on him.

In Chinatown I liked the tea shops and candy shops, not to eat (my uncle enjoys the dried octopus snacks) so much as to wonder at. My cousin bought a silk halter top, "for clubbing if he'll let me out of the house," and I bought a cotton robe with symbols on it. She's the blonde and I'm the brunette. Then we went to the aquarium.

"Sturgeon! Yum!" I have never been to an aquarium with someone who wanted to eat everything. Then on the way back to the cabin we picked up Dungeness crab and clams and mussels and my uncle made that San Francisco-style stew with sourdough for dinner. We ate outside. I hardly ever look at the sky, but my uncle looked up, crossing his legs and sipping his wine. My uncle was getting pretty drunk, which at first comes off like he's a little pleased with himself, lightening up, but then he starts to get psychological. He went into the cabin, we heard the *zip*, *zip* of his bags, and he came back out with a star chart. I don't know anything about stars. He waved the chart and said, "Speaking of child abuse…" and my cousin got up from the table and went inside and came back with an extra shirt to put on. My uncle said, "Remember how we used to look at the stars?" and my cousin said, "Dad, put the chart away" and put the shirt on. He would not let up on the subject. I couldn't tell what he wanted me to do, if it was a test involving whether or not I'd think the star chart was cool. I cleared some dishes and he followed me into the kitchen with the star chart. It was yellow, with two parts that revolved in relation to each other.

I could just see it, though, because he's a lot like my own father, tottering after me, shaking me by the shoulders, saying, "Goddamn you girl, why aren't you following in my footsteps?" My cousin and I have talked about how I'm not going to have kids for my reasons and she's not going to have kids for her reasons. We look at each other and know we're the end of the line.

HER SUICIDE

After her father killed himself, one thing she wanted to know was which gun. Possibly the hunting and guarding gun they kept in the house and all learned with. Probably that was the gun, but she thought maybe, in the most considerate way, he might have gone and got a different gun, to clarify the event.

METH

On the road to ruin a man in the maroon car was on meth and driving like it. The girls lagged behind for safety. A couple days later they saw him at the store with a boy and a puppy. A.J. got nervous. She didn't know where to put her eyes. The puppy was so cute. The boy was eating out of a plastic bag and the man was carrying the puppy. They crossed paths on the porch of the store. Behind them was the beautiful landscape. The man wasn't carrying any groceries, but then they were all on their way back toward the maroon car. The man carried, carried, and carried the puppy. He was a little handsome. Maybe the man didn't have teeth. The boy was cuter with every bite. Give me a break, this is not the end of the world.

Kim had said, as they were parking next to the maroon car, "That's that car from before that almost killed us." It had gone up and down the curves in the mountain road as if there weren't curves, just straight ahead on methamphetamines. They saw his teeth for a second and they still seemed pretty okay. One thing A.J. always knew was if she lost her job, without dental she'd finally start flossing like clockwork. They went up the stairs onto the porch of the store. Kim said to the boy, "Is that good?"

and the boy nodded with a lot of energy. Kim patted the puppy's head in the man's arms. Then, in the store, she started looking at the shelves. That was about it. Puppies and little children.

Live and let live? Down at the breakfast shack a man is eating a breakfast burrito and he's the father of a kid he beat, who another lady in the town adopted, and they all live *here*. A.J. felt angry. *I am not adopting that boy and that puppy!* she thought as she passed by them with her purchases, bags swiping the door of his car.

TAKEN

My father got really into UFOs. He'd talk about it at dinner, about how he wanted to be taken. I'd be freaked out that Martians were going to take my dad, and he'd sit there with the chicken and pout because when would he get taken already. He'd had a vasectomy and they have to do those experiments. There was always a sense that something was going to happen in the house. There was real fear of poverty. Always bomb-shelter mode, the stocking of the shelves with cans of food, because my father had grown up super poor, so he'd be really afraid if there weren't enough peas on the shelf in the garage. Like we had two refrigerators and he had to see a certain *height* of food. I have a lot more fear as I get older. My parents were half-assed about both their religions, so that trickled down to about a quarter, but it did its job. I was freaked out about the scapula and the Lord's prayer. The string for around your neck is piece-of-shit pleather and one night it broke and I remember just lying in bed putting the string on top of me. Evidence I was trying. A ticket stub. Airplanes when they crash, they just go down and down. Like because you bought that ticket. It's the way they keep going down that gets me. Maybe they made that phone call to their loved one.

I never want the apocalypse to happen.

Polar bears clinging to ice, all that shit, my worst nightmare. Being separated. I am so afraid of not being together.

HALF

For half of the year, when her father was working, it was as if she weren't half made of him. But during the summer he worked on the car in the garage, and she'd play near his feet with bolts, stubby screwdrivers, the ratchet and its sockets, and the wrench that looked like a dinosaur. He cursed a lot, headless and heartless, but not at her. She knew all the tools, and when he called, she handed each into the dark, grit from the garage floor pressing into her legs. The holes in her father's jeans, her father's sandals, the hair on his toes, the all-around blankness of his feet, his voice, bouncing and metallic, distant and safe, the general quiet mess, all there beyond her eyes.

When she comes home from school on the day of the apocalypse she's fifteen. The garage door has closed on her father. Waist down he is in the driveway. The rest of him is in the garage. The garage is suddenly a mouth that has shut already. She thinks of the mysterious fall of the dinosaurs. She thinks of the movie *Captains Courageous*, which they watched together, she and her father, on late night TV, and she remembers the pleasure of being included in his insomnia, this new other half of sleep, looking at the side of his face in the television light, like watching someone sleep, like being a ghost. Spencer Tracy bobbed among sharks, truncated in the water. They'd been reading "Ozymandias" in school, and she was still thinking about the word *trunk*. They'd been talking about Persephone, the pomegranate, and the two ways people tended to pronounce her name. In grammar, they were going back to tenses because nobody seemed to get it after all. "You're slipping!" said the teacher. Her father lay far away in a new way: something about viewpoint, something about organizing principles, something about presence, absence, something.

THREE SISTERS: BLOND, BRUNETTE, REDHEAD

We were coming out of the movies into some real-life darkness when we heard his coat open. Rows and rows of apocalypses shone along the satin lining. He blocked our way with his wide stance. "Pssst, wanna buy a—" he hissed, but I held my hands over my younger sister's ears.

"I've got something for you," he snarled and was about to reveal his you-know-what but my older sister clamped her hands over our younger sister's eyes. He stomped, thwarted. We could hardly see the shape of him in the darkness, we had no idea how to locate his vulnerable features in all that swirling fabric, the edges of the apocalypses winking in and out of view confusingly, and our hands were all used up on the little one, besides.

"You fuckers! You apocalyptical—" (or did he say "apocalyptic little"? or did he say "of all the people will you"? It's hard to know what comes to me glazed with my preoccupations…) His hands reached down at us from his great height and we all clumped together, trying to shut him out with our bodies, knowing we were bound for the interior of his coat unless we could somehow pin down his head or his hands or his—

SAILS, HULL, JIBS

She was eating an enormous salad at an outdoor café at the marina. Every few bites she bent under the table to rearrange a folded napkin under one of its three feet. She added a bottle cap under a second foot. The third foot hovered. Then she scooched the table around on the cement. She took another few bites of the salad, which loomed like a mountain in front of her. She could see her knees through the mottled glass tabletop. The top wobbled in its white metal frame. She looked around, feeling the edges of panic. A boat made a shape against the sky, a triangle with potential dimension. Everyone seemed happy as bunnies. Bunches ate, clinking glasses. She turned sharply in her chair, this way and then the other way. A few people looked up. Her breath felt like a train. More people looked up. A boat went by. It was a marina on the harbor and still she could see only one boat. It went by, sails gushing, and by the time she couldn't see it anymore everyone in the café had turned to watch her as, item by item, signposts, trashcans, pedestrians, and then, plank by plank, the pier, disappeared, until she was sitting with her salad in a desert at the ocean surrounded by nothing but suspended eyes.

ARTISTS

When artists transport the furnishings of a family room into a gallery space and paint everything white, they are trying to transform contents into ash without using fire. Results include: knitted afghan, previously fuzzy and multicolored; oversized patriarch chair with pop-out footrest and sweat-catchers on the head and armrests like sugared pancakes; the fireplace of brick; television, huge-assed or flat-screen, depending on the era, oozing spray-snow; shag carpet turned frothy white sea, as frozen in paint as the sea within us; the bookcase of books arranged with knick-knacks from around the world, little children with outfits that used to be the colors of national flags—but back to the books, because what else in the room might have something still comprehensible there on the *inside*? (That sea?) Perhaps if you crack open the popcorn on the coffee table it will reveal a GM seed within a seed beyond its coating.

I remember when we finished remodeling the house, we'd covered every surface with another polymer, and then we found out about the plumbing in the cement. We're supposed to raise a family in this sack of shit. Artists do this all the time—cover the surface, cover like news, like the opposite of oil. These artists with their white paint are signifying ash to make a post-apocalyptic space. It's because of where they came from: earth. Coating the things with paint erases and exposes them like you can't make your mind up. When we are with the artists I'm thinking of, our throats have filled with cotton to help us be ourselves even when bisected. As painted things float further from their meanings, we can too. When everything is coated with the debris of everything else it has the appeal of a finished product.

HOT TICKET

In my town, where we live on a hill in the desert which was a desert even before this last apocalypse, I can stand on the wall surrounding the house and look down with binoculars. Tonight there is a famous rock band in the ball park. Everyone left is watching them hook up their amplifiers to some car batteries they found. The band is in leather outfits, just like the old days, like nothing happened, except now they don't have roadies.

They're being really particular about tuning their instruments, given the circumstances, always close to starting and then not starting. Rumor has it they sold tickets to every single person left on earth. That's like 100. Except us. We're up on the hill. Behind the wall. With my binoculars. Looking down on the rock stars. No way am I paying for this show.

AUDIENCE

I would sit in the back seat and everything we were passing—street signs, buildings, trees, animals—I was as still as a telephone pole, and they rushed past me. I personified them all so they'd been packing up and preparing. I was a stone in a river, and all of these things were fleeing whatever was happening. I would imagine what each of them would sound like as they were telling me that they were leaving.

The pitch of their voice, or how they would say "Goodbye!" or if they were similar things, two buildings that looked alike, would they sound the same or different, or a grouping of several things together, of trees, would they speak in unison? They were rushing past me this way, calling out, but I didn't feel afraid.

They weren't warning me, they were just getting out of there as fast as possible, but I was headed into there, and I was going to be the only one there when I got there, whatever it was. But no, I wasn't afraid.

I'll be back in a sec. Do you want one of those sandwiches?

The thing with the rocking chair is, my mother told me that when she was a toddler, she had a rocking chair that she would sit in for hours, and I found a picture of it in with these funny-smelling relics from the '60s, like Clark Gable picturebooks. My mom looks Asian but she's not Asian, and when she was little she looked even more Asian, even with her eyes, blue like mine, which of course you can't tell in the picture, and it's always strange to see your mother shrunken into this distant person—and when she got on this kick, she sat me down, sometimes me and my brother, but usually just me, my brother wouldn't sit for such things, but she would sit cross-legged, really tall, on the couch or anything, and she would rock back and forth like this and tell me terrible things. About all her child abuse, about the Holocaust, about all the people who died in her family —

No, no, no one's Jewish or anything—

But what terrible fates happened to all of them, she'd get into this trance state, rocking. About wanting to kill her father when he was dying. I remember my parents were still together, I remember the house we lived in, my mom rocking in this trance and telling me about all the terrible things because her family was just nothing but terrible things, just misery, misery, misery, my dad's family too, they're just miserable people and miserable things happen to them, and I became really depressed and despondent, all I could do was cry about all these stories. But in this one house I remember my dad intervened—he rarely did, his strategy usually was to be gone, to be at work all the time—so he was at home and I remember he said, "Pamela," because he always called her Pamela, "what are you telling her that for?" He took me to the grocery store to buy groceries and he was trying to cheer me up by offering me funny stories from his side of the family. I just sobbed. It doesn't work like that. I'd make her tell me again because I was afraid I'd forget them. She handed me this thing and I felt like I had to take care of it.

I always thought my mom was inappropriate. When anybody tells me something as if I am an audience, as if I am not the person I am, who they know as person—oh, ick, there's sand in this glass. Do you want to go swimming later, when it's dark?

But when somebody tells me something as if I am an audience—

Because I could have been anyone, her daughter, the mailman, the dog, it was just her subjecting you to whatever—

I'd get home, she'd get home from work, and I'd have to sit in the bathroom while she was taking a shit or something, and I'd just sit there on the bathroom floor and listen to her talk about whatever.

You don't feel like an audience, right? You sure?

She was the oldest of the kids, her dad had polio, he was in a wheelchair, her mother went off to work so she was left tending to all the kids and being the surrogate sex partner to her father, so she—my mother didn't have a chance in the world to not be crazy, there was nothing leading up to her adult life that didn't insure she was going to be batshit crazy, and I know that. That is a sad tale, that woman. My brother came home with a permission slip about the Holocaust and for a while that was the show, my mother pontificating on the horrors of the Holocaust, the horrors of the world and all of history, it was a show, explaining to us that Hitler pretty much wiped out anyone who didn't have blond hair and blue eyes, not explaining to a child about genocide, and I can remember it, sitting in the family room, and she's rocking back and forth, and my only way of wrapping my head around that and putting myself in relationship to it was saying "I'm so glad we have blue eyes." How can I feel safe? Oh, I have blue eyes. Then she went back to the Holocaust. She just walked out of such garbage, such garbage, and then tried to make a life out of it. I have an amazing memory, but you know I can't even remember what state she lives in now. Oh wow, do you see that, that thing? What is it, a tornado over the water? It's pretty.

TAHITI

Instead of the mood of the light from the kitchen in the dark in the heat with the fronds from her limber plants at her elbows suggesting Tahiti in the old days of painters now on coffee cups, she hoped a sheen would ease across her imagination even as the Earth fell away, as the animals died, as the fields fumed, as the turnips in the refrigerator shriveled into the faces of old ladies like the one she would become if she only waited. It took something psychic to refrain from relaxing into one of the voices in the town that flattened real life. She took a piece of ice into her mouth and let it hurt, perhaps the last ice on earth. She took a look at the house and felt pickled. She turned her mind toward the several moments in her history that were worth considering, and watched the ideas turn in the atmosphere like model planets and then fail. Home, home, home is where you used to think you wanted to go.

CONJUGATIONS

The perpetrators arrived to offer statements for the record.

Nature looked amazing in a cloak. "Because I know better. Because of what you did to the good and the beautiful." God assented from a cloud.

The human looked desperate and unfashionable. "Because my power made me evil. I mean, I saw God in a beaker, and clearly he's in a cloud. I mean my troubled childhood. I mean my charisma or insanity."

The alien phased in and out of view and the voice in waves of particles came through. "I am from the sea, or the stars, the past, the future, your silly hands, your body microscopically against you... When I am sentient, when I am animal... When I am phenomena... So honestly, fuck you."

But when pressed, each eventually confessed: I was in class. In class I was often lost and did not know what to do. But one day the teacher called on me, and, astonished, I *knew*. Apocalypto. Apocalypteis. Apocalyptei. Apocalyptomen. Apocalyptete. Apocalyptousi. At last I had something to offer.

III.
THROUGH TO THREE
QUARTERS OF A HUNDRED
APOCALYPSES

implosion, the crumpling of paper

THE OTHER WAY AROUND

We came at last to the wackily fantastic land of opposites. We'd read this one in childhood. Candy tasted terrible and we all wanted liver with onions. Water got us drunk and we could only breathe when we were under it. Right was wrong, so we were very popular. Our mouths swapped spots with our assholes. Our belly buttons turned outward (except for George's) and our vaginas, well, you had to be there. The birds under our feet annoyed us with their philosophies. It was the end of all we'd known, and our hopes sank.

NICE DAY

A lot of things are happening around the world, and happening in patterns that if you read a book, the book will point out to you, chapter by chapter, the exact way the patterns are happening here, here, and here. You can feel like you're learning something for a while but then as soon as you catch on, you think, *If I keep reading this book is it just going to be more examples?* Then as the book is rising and falling on your belly you see the light from the window, leafy dapples, so pretty. You feel a little lonely but then you remember that reading feeling of being *on to* something, those early pages. You pick it back up but now the book takes a turn for a paragraph into a sort of rhetoric that pisses you off, and that seems to give rise to another sort of tension connected to loneliness because you're afraid you might abandon the book for good and all your hopes for what it might have given you—and that just makes you masturbate.

The efficient orgasm is the most productive moment of the day, because, apocalyptically, it has wiped the slate clean, and no one will ever know about it. What are you going to do now? Most of the time you could go back to reading. Some of the time you fantasize about a ragtag group of strangers thrown together by circumstance who go on a quest for some orgasm big enough to leave them wanting something *different* than they wanted before.

Like what? Gross food? Ugly stuff? Feeling like crap? Not understanding anything?

All you do is lie in bed with no underwear, trying to think of something better and better. In your next fantasy you are lying in moist dirt and leaves, in exactly the same position. In your next fantasy you are lying in hot sand, but no book. In your next fantasy, an old standby, you are running, you have a flag on a stick that means something, you are faster than all the animals, everything is burning in your wake, you're truly awake, the flames are taking on the shapes of everyone you've ever heard of in a herd behind you. They are overtaking you. In a last gasp you're engulfed. It's the kind of thing that leaves real people scarred for life.

HANGINGS

Already this year he had inherited the clothes of two famous dead people. At least one had killed himself, and he knew both tertiarily. This current one, a third, was his wife's mentor, and he and his wife had gone to visit the widow where she'd holed up in a house by the sea. In evening light, the dead mentor's wife looked at his wife across the broad planks of the table, in a room filled with rugs and masks from around the world.

He was walking around looking at the masks while the women were talking quietly when he heard the woman say something to his wife about his "frame." He thought about picture frames—was his body a frame, or was his body *in* a frame (skin as frame?); was his skeleton his frame, and what's that all about, inner beauty, what you hang it on? There was framed art in other rooms of the house, but in this room it was just the masks. He thought about his face: his brain behind his face thinking about his face. He was not good with people the way his wife was, but he was just as smart. There were a lot of good places to hang yourself in this house, though he knew it had happened at the place in the city.

"At least have him try the suits," the wife of his wife's mentor was saying. "They're here, in the closet upstairs." Hanging, everyone thought. "I have someone for the sweaters," she said. He thought of himself in the dead man's sweaters, perhaps six of them one over another, gray and brown, bulging, soundproofing his chest. He had the sweaters of another famous man already, buried in a closet in the hall at home.

The man who'd been promised the sweaters had been there for brunch. Now he stood in the hedges watching the women talk and the man poke his finger into the eye of a mask and touch the wall behind it. The man in the hedges had been in the same cohort as the wife. They'd been rivals for the mentor's attention and occasional lovers, and the dead mentor had used them to challenge each other. The dead mentor had often been unfaithful to his wife. The mentor's wife had been unfaithful to him only once, years before her husband even started up with his conduct, and this had been with the man in the hedges. At lunch, the man in the hedges had said, "All I want are his sweaters. I loved him too, you know. Not like you, but he was a very important figure in my life." The word *figure* hung in the room, under the broad rough roof beams. A breeze came up the dunes, through the hedges and the window, and sketched squiggly lines around their heads. She thought about the word *figure*, about her body, what it could possibly mean to reason with it, with the body, once and for all. Only after he'd hung himself did so many people he'd fucked come out of the woodwork. Men, women, old people, young people. Loved, too, she suspected, some of them. Her husband had had a lot of meaning, she kept being reminded. She'd told the man in the hedges, as she put marmalade onto a muffin she was not going to eat, that she'd think about the sweaters or if there might be a better choice for him. "A special book?" she suggested. "A piece of art? Something small?" The man said that back in the day you could smoke, and the mentor had worn his sweaters and smoked all through class, letting butts pile up on the floor by his chair in the seminar room, so involved with what his students were thinking that it never crossed his mind to use the ashtray that sat on the table next to the case for his glasses. "That's what it's all about, in the end," he'd said to the wife. "What we've done to each other up *here*." He tapped the side of his head, *tap*, *tap*, as if it were fruit. The wife couldn't help it: "Figures," she said. She'd be glad for him to take the sweaters.

The women faced each other across the broad plank table. The man in the hedges watched them through the window, comparing the women's bodies to each other, and his own body to the body of the other man, who took a mask off the wall and put it over his face and scanned the room through its eyes. The women looked deeper and deeper into each other's eyes. They both started to well up with emotion. They reached their hands across the table to each other. One of them sniffed, to shake the feeling. The other one said, "Where were we?" Then the man in the mask saw the man in the window and yelped. He dropped the mask and it bounced once and then wobbled like a coin, but when he shot his eyes back to the window, he didn't see anything except the hedge, the reflection of the globe of a lamp, the moon above, and the dunes beyond it. He'd almost forgotten they were by the sea. He looked down at the mask and thought it must have made him see something that hadn't really been there. *Hang it all*, he thought. He'd never met the dead man, but he felt a longing for him when he looked at those women so deep in each other's eyes, so filled with longing. It made him want, very much, to have the suits or anything else the dead man had left to offer. He looked forward to wearing them as any other clothes are worn, into the future, time doing its quiet business along the seams.

THIEF

A thief crawled in through my window and took a bunch of my stuff, but I wasn't alarmed, because he looked so familiar with all his fingers, the dark outfit, the apocalyptic two-by-two of his limbs, eyes, nostrils, the all-over symmetry of his presentation, one foot in front of the other like a good soldier. The thief was like everyone I've ever met (except Billy, because of the accident on top of the genetic condition.)

Now my friends want me to question my empty house, but I recognize it as mine as well as when it was full of all that stuff I brought in from other places, like where I shopped, and when I got presents for my birthday.

Besides, I owe, I know. How much do you have to change before you are no longer yourself? You can change everything, and you will never get away.

You know what I did? I offered the thief a whiskey. The thief drank whiskey with me in the night. We stood on the balcony and watched my neighbors' cats walk along fences. We watched shadows move all by themselves. "Look," he said. "It's practically us." I couldn't see where he was pointing, but surely he was right. He let the sack slip and it spilled open with relief. We looked at each other among my shimmering things, and merged.

PARABLE IN TRANSATLANTIC

I was in a play. Sharing a role was part of the concept. We knew only that much at casting.

We'd had the script for a week, but as usual I had not even started to memorize my lines even though I kept studying them. The other actress cast as me already knew them cold, was already making choices. I was there for rehearsal along with a spotty crowd. Who are these people already? During a break, standing in the audience, I had a face-to-face with the director.

"It's our first rehearsal," I said. "I think it's really unfair to let the public watch when the cast hasn't even had a read-through." The director said no one else seemed to mind. I suspected a hidden-camera-documentary aspect.

I put on my transatlantic and said, "But you know as well as I, first reads are intimate." The other actress was up there on the wooden planks of the stage, a redhead with a nothing-fancy mode of expression, and she was playing around with one of our monologues like I wasn't there, mouthing and gesturing absently with her styrofoam coffee cup, a napkin stuffed in it, poking out over the lip. I was worried about sharing this role with her, because I could tell I was wearing my mother's face. The director was gazing into his own consciousness, maybe or maybe not in regard to the point I was trying to make. On impulse I said to him, "Does this face make me look old? Does it make me too old for this part?" Now he swung around to me like I was crossing a line, so I said, "Come on, I thought we were doing theater here." He looked like someone famous, but I was actually more famous than he, in our circle. Now I was even thinking in transatlantic. He clapped his hands and everyone on the stage stopped what they were doing and turned to face the rest of us. Some of them were in the audience by this point, and some of the audience was wandering around on the stage. Everyone was in street clothes, and about half of us had the same cups.

"In this story," the director said, and everyone leaned in, "in addition to what you know already, we are all going to play each other's parts. We are all going to play each other as if we were each other, and we are going to play each other as if we were each other's parts. If you are still worried about being someone else too much, this will be a challenge for you. I want you all to keep in mind what I'm saying, but don't let it show. I want you to keep your own face, because we'll be working as a group." Suddenly the nothing-fancy redheaded girl was one of many, and everyone in the cast was trying to look at everyone else at once. I was trying so hard I could feel my brain through my face. I wanted to do what he was asking. I was really inspired at the time. You remember what that's like, don't you? Not feeling in public at all? We forgot about them entirely, even though they were mixed up with us; we just went for it. And all through the process I really tried to ditch my hang-ups the more we all got into the piece and into each other. But I kind of suspect the show sucked. My mother came, and she's not one to mince words. In fact, she came with my ex because they're still friends, in fact sometimes I think they might be more than friends, whatever that is, and people should be with the people that work for them I guess. It's about timing. There might have been a time when the people I love could watch me in a show like that, but I probably would have been too involved with them to do a good job. Now I think I did a good job, being and not being myself and others in a group. But I sure don't know how anyone else felt about it.

WAYS OF LEARNING

Deeper in history than anyone knew, furrowed in a grayed-out land-scape, bees lined up, humming, along the branches of a cluster of trees, and as their noise and their wings began to make the leaves tingle, the sun moved along the other side of the earth, which operated as a hunk between the scene and the sun. The longer they hummed, the more they seemed to pulse, because sounds were forming patterns, which is exactly what happens when matter meets matter and time passes. You can hear pulses separate themselves into words and land on things as bees land on things. If the things nod back across the bees to you, there is a theory we can learn being demonstrated.

LIBRARY

At the buffet I responded in the way I thought this guy wanted me to respond. A moment later, once I absorbed what he'd actually said, I was no longer sure how I felt about it. Now I have forgotten what it was. I regrouped and withdrew to the balcony. I noticed that if I agreed with this woman, she would assume we were both familiar with the article, and I could watch esteem growing in her eyes the more silent I became.

All in all, really I only give the library lip service, and when I say "library" I mean the library and everything it stands for, regarding knowledge. I want to give props to the library, for holding out, but really I never go. There's a dictionary in my bedroom, for what it's worth.

You can get away with almost anything by nodding or asking an honest question. People love it when you don't know something. That's something to contribute to society. I've heard about books about endless libraries. I've listened on and on about books about infinity. Sometimes I get caught up in the math, books duplicating internally and externally. There are insects that are born pregnant—look it up. It's as if the books in the library are just books with nothing in them except more books.

The thing about the library I come back to is that so far it exists, like people exist, which is not a given. I come back to this right when I'm in the bedroom pushing the coats around, looking for that one coat I came with. I push through coats as if they're skins of the people they came from, just too much to deal with, I'm just pushing through them. They're really the skins off animals and other people's backs. They're really just ideas. In fact the library is there just like all the things I'll probably never do with my mind or my body, like ride in a hot air balloon or stab someone with a bayonet or have sex with two hotties at once or advanced gymnastics, in fact most sports, or access conviction, matter, or the metaphysical.

LOOK INSIDE

If she worries about the lint in her belly button she will look for it with her finger. As if her finger is a one-eyed monster, she'll look for the lint and scratch for it with the monster's one tooth (the tooth that covers its eye like a lid) and she'll be able to feel the link between her navel and her clitoris. When she's worried about lint in her belly button it's bad news, she only got there through deep neurotic space, and her skin is so hot and so sensitive that almost any sort of poking around can cause irritation. What a head up your ass, what a snake and tail, what navel-gazing, rash, infection, lonely and unfortunate forms of creation. The world is an incubator. You can see its progeny working its way into her orifices. You can see her in her bathroom now, plugging herself with cotton, virile, viral, sterilizing. Take a look at yourself. Look inside. With the onset of nanotechnology the new frontier is in you, autobiography is the quest literature of our time, and almost everyone has begun to throw up, row after row, whether they know it or not. Luckily the throw-up is stop-motioned before it can get ugly.

THE NEW ME

They could stay afloat for only so long. Before the deranged creatures picked them off. They were so thirsty or so hungry. They swirled in the raging wind, fire, and water. Their skin shriveled. Time had ended and yet passed. Parched, they watched the last particles of moisture rise and fade in the golden air above an earth of previously unknown colors. They trudged on and on but the land was barren. Fungus rotted their limbs and bacteria new to the dying world cruised their organs. Germs, maggots, and death from virile viral microscopic life loomed in the near future. Buildings tumbled upon them. Flying debris severed them. Chasms opened wide and swallowed. They were crushed and strewn, and they exploded. Their brains burst from the noise. A spinning cow or lamp broke them. Their insides fell out. Their fingers crumbled. The inside of my skin was the earth, and grass took root and grew toward my heart. I had drunk and eaten enough pesticides to make it possible. My organs, robotic as zombies, worked with what they got. I saw myself clumping about, dribbling clippings from my razor-sharp teeth, pulsing with quotations.

BEN AND BECKY HAVE WORDS

That day they were blowing off work in rented kayaks and wasting it by having a fight. Now they were in the silence that comes when articulate people can't make anything move with their vocabulary. Chirping, lapping, the bridge in the distance like a fake frown. The city lagged behind. Below, they had to rely on their imaginations for fish. Becky thought of a recent moment on the internet with Singleton Copey's *Watson and the Shark*, inspired by an event that took place in Havana, Cuba, in 1749. Fourteen-year-old Brook Watson, an orphan serving as a crew member on a trading ship, was attacked by a shark while swimming alone in the harbor. His shipmates, who had been waiting on board to escort their captain ashore, launched a valiant rescue effort. But it seemed from the painting that the effort was in vain. As a child she'd thought that boy was a girl with beautiful flowing blonde hair, arching before the shark's wide mouth in the waves, the shark's tail so distant it might have been another shark. Two men reached for her in matching white shirts.

A woman with beautiful flowing brown hair lunged at the shark with a spear. A black man stood behind the woman with the spear, compositionally parallel to the girl in the water. He was in his own world. He was above the fray, both interested and feeling something Becky could never quite peg. People in the boat were exhibiting fear, sadness, bravery, but one thing you don't always think of is joining the victim.

Now, Becky had always loved the lip service of a good internet citation. When she cut and pasted into her own documents it made her feel like it was a free country. This, she felt, is how you make something real of your own. Copley himself had made three versions of the paintings, after all, and just turned the "Borghese Gladiator" on its side for the figure of Watson. But just as she was deciding on a way to bring the painting up with Ben, he spat some mean shit at her and she spat something back. Then, while Ben was trying to come up with another example of what he meant, she got down to her skivvies and slipped into the water. This surprised him so much that he dropped his paddle overboard. A shark came by and ate it in one fell swoop. Ben screamed something about being up a creek, and that's when she called him the enemy of expression.

DREAM MATERIAL

It was before there were tall buildings in Mexico City, but there were tall buildings, and flying vehicles. High and gray. Concrete. Nothing organic. No neon lights. A sensation of falling, maybe sweat, maybe an earthquake and Tlatelolco, this huge housing project where I lived right before the big one in '85. One of the buildings came down and killed a thousand people with cheap concrete, just like the other day in practically name your country, it can happen any day.

Opus caementicium made the Pantheon possible.

After the apocalypse, I see concrete. I can tell you a lot about concrete in developing countries. You add water to stretch it and that's our downfall, a concrete downfall. I can't say "developing" without irony. I can't say "concrete."

DREAM HOUSE

My wife and I finally chose an architect we'd admired for years, a guy who had gone to our college, though we'd only known him from afar. He impressed us. He'd always been artistic. He did the drawing and we did the dreaming. Natural efficient everything, modest and modernist, we wanted that balance of cutting edge and built to last. We were excited and scared—we had good money, but it was still a lot. We told friends over dinner about our plans, going over the idea, couple after couple. We ended up describing that house at practically every restaurant in town that we liked. Real estate, figurative estate. I just thought of that!

We'd had friends fuck up in process. One couple bought a house, turned out to be made of stuff called *hardboard*. Well, they learned via lawsuit that it was not *designed* to hold up in the *rain*. Thirty year mortgage and ten years life expectancy on the *siding*. Just imagine all the replacing you're expected to do on a dream like that. What is it about cells, they all slough and replace within seven years? I once thought of a reason why that must be an urban legend, but now I forget. It must have been right before falling asleep, or that instant waking up, disappearing and reappearing to myself.

Don't worry, we didn't split, we're fine.

At these dinners we described the blueprints. We drew on napkins. Our friends kept saying, "People want the master bedroom to be a suite.

People want a garage. People want a stove the size of a tank. His and hers everything." At dinner, I'd say, "but this is our dream house. It's not *people's* dream house."

Later my wife would say things she never would have said before. "We should have a real laundry, we should have a proper foyer." In a marriage you learn to see it the other person's way. We'd spread the blueprint across the table in the rental. Her eyes going over the lines, my eyes going over the lines. I was placing our belongings in the house, and I could see her placing little people-friends walking around in there among our belongings. Lines such as countertops. Vessels such as vases. I ran my eyes along my wife. It was inevitable. Are you my dream, are you mine, what are you, who are you for?

Programmatic inflation, our architect called it, when he'd redrafted according to what we'd heard about these buyers our friends imagined. We built the house. It was over budget, but you know that going in. We didn't fight about what happened to our dream house, but we definitely alluded to it. "Where are his *boundaries*," she'd say about some guy at work, and I have to believe we both felt the house in there. "What did you dream?" I'd ask her in the morning. I knew the house was in what I was saying. A couple of times, alone in the house we built, I've even felt the real house like an invisible balloon around me. One time I felt it I really laughed at myself because if there's one thing I have ever excelled at in life it's being in this institution we call marriage. Another time, I remembered following my mother on a tour of a great house in some state, not where we lived—probably Monticello. Suffice to say, my parents did not have a marriage like mine. It had been a long drive on a very hot day. My dad was so angry he was not joining us, he was waiting in the car. In the tour group I was at everyone's hips. I almost fell asleep walking behind my mother's bottom to the tour guide's speech, my mother's bottom in her summer pants blooming white up the staircase toward the great dome.

DREAM GIRL

She was so excited about the present she had decided to get me that she told me what it was going to be. I loved it. It was a great idea for a present and just right for me. It was what I had been dreaming of without even knowing it. But time rolled on and I didn't get the present itself. Of course, this is all in the past. Now she's gone. Big surprise. I don't even get pleasure from the idea of the present anymore, because I was so mad about her not actually getting the present that I forgot what it was going to be. I can joke about the eternal present of the thought that counts, but what I'm actually trying to give you is an understanding of the stasis of certain forms of pain. It's a matter of eradication.

FEELINGS

I smoothed the described sheet over the described person I'd loved before the apocalypse. The rich feelings welled from the page. Under the blanket, the person I loved remained. We used to mean so much.

FOR REAL

Slowly, carefully, gingerly, I began to suspect I remained ironical.

SPACE AND TIME

He went to an exhibit of photographs of people standing goofily with iconic art. They had their arms around it, sat in its lap. They used their fingers for mustaches, exploiting perspective. They got bawdy. The people interacted with the art in the photos within a range that included mean-spirited, grimly reverent, and trying to make it stop bugging them. It's not like he felt looking at art was one thing, but in his thoughts he was participating in a millennial chain of erasure. In the final room was a hologram of a statue surrounded by holograms of people pointing at the art, surrounded by people hopping around like monkeys, surrounded by people pointing at the people who were acting like monkeys. All the figures were strobing from 3-D color representations to black-and-white 2-D representations. There was some kind of algorithm about which figures were represented in which way through a sequence. You could walk in among the holograms, probably, but he didn't get that far, because that's when his wife called him from the Everglades, where she was hunting anacondas that had washed from homes in the hurricane and taken over. She'd read all about it on the internet and flown down to help like Sean Penn. "An anaconda has *exploded* from swallowing an alligator its same size," she whispered. "I am looking at this spectacle as we speak. I am up to my knees." She was British and that still made her sound authoritative on nature. "It's so *Jurassic*, so *diasporic*. When an anaconda begins to *miscalculate* in this manner..." she said, her voice quavering within the uneven reception.

The museum was filling with rowdy viewers challenging the taped lines around the spaces taken up by holograms, and his anxiety rose in concert with their increasing numbers. "I love you," he whispered into the phone, right as someone jostled him and his glasses went askew. For a moment, the Braque in the next gallery cohered. By the time he'd righted them and slipped into a quiet corner, he'd lost the connection with his wife. He texted her furtively. "I love you." He spelled the whole thing out, for emphasis. But someone jostled him again and this time his glasses fell off and his phone slid away from him, like a comet, into the depths of the exhibit.

WHAT I GOT

I cleared the kitchen island and placed upon it the brown paper bag that contained my three purchases. It had been such a long time since I'd had a good day shopping, since before the banks collapsed, before the oil spill. In the new era of being careful I'd been keeping an eye out for, among other things, the *perfect* bag, a *perfect* bag for me for carrying things around in, and I finally found it! A glossy black one you can tell might be made from recycled materials—but not obvious in any way that would become dated—and with the right amount of pockets, so you don't lose things in the bag and you don't lose things in the pockets. I took it, along with my additional items, out of the brown paper grocery-style shopping bag with stiff twine handles they'd placed it in, and I placed it, in its silver tissue wrapping, on the ice-white and recently de-crumbed surface, unrolled it like a body from a carpet. I set the new bag aside for the moment, as I am one who eats the tips of pies last.

Then I spread the silver tissue. What a satisfying feeling against the outer edges of my hands, like what I still do and have done all my life with my hands across the surface of the water in my bathtub every chance I get—what a day! take me away! Across the water I make the gesture of a conjurer, like I could make something rise. Then I folded the tissue into a square the size of a picnic napkin and put it into a bag of other pretty paper in the closet in the hallway for the future. Then I lifted the brown paper bag by its twine, shook it against the air, and pinched it at the folds. The bag made a huge noise in the quiet apartment in the silent weekday complex. I thought of a mountain crumbling between the tectonic plates of history. It was almost six o'clock. Everyone in the universe was caught in rush hour except me. I tried to hold on to the feeling I had when I left work for lunch and did not go back.

I repeated the process with my remaining purchases. Folding tissue into square, putting tissue into bag. Green tissue with a print of tiny crowns in glittery green. Inside, a jeweled pillbox. Blue tissue slick on one side and natural on the other. Inside, a silk scarf with a pattern of peacock plumes.

I carried the jeweled pillbox in the palm of my hand into the bathroom and filled it with an assortment: a couple Sudafed, a couple Advil, a couple Ambien, Xanax, Anaprox, Multi-Daily, golden Omega fatty acid fish oil caplets. You know how colorful and artfully shaped pills are. I returned to the kitchen, my formica island, and put the pillbox into the new black bag along with my ratty wallet. I smoothed the silk scarf across the island. I wrapped it around my head and tied it at the nape of my neck. I felt exotic. I put the strap of my new bag over my shoulder and put my hand on it where it rested at my hip, like I was ready for action.

What a slick crap apartment, thrown up in the boom. What shiny new things.

I remembered the fable from childhood with the cock on the cat on the donkey on the road. They were musicians running away from destitute lives to be in a band together. My purchases, one, two, three. My head in a purchase, my purchases in my hand. I gazed at the popcorn so-called cathedral ceiling above the island and thought of the sky above it, my skull and bones below, my painted feathers a layer in between. I decided to take a spin around the neighborhood. I'd taken this risk, ditching work. I wanted to know if I felt empty or fulfilled.

I walked like a wandering mind around the neighborhood, feeling out my new things among blocks below highways, whistling my favorite tune (*you're toxic, I'm slipping under...*) until I came upon a vacant lot surrounded by chain link overflowing with thistles. I hardly ever had the chance to walk around the neighborhood, so the last time I'd seen it it'd been a desert in there, and now it was completely filled with the hugest possible thistles, just glorious, elbowing each other on the way up, spines shining, purple heads like muppets and dragons, this overflowing of weeds, this *life* pouring out over the chain link. The history of the lot was a drug den got torn down after a grassroots victory, but then because of something to do with property taxes the lot was sitting there foreclosed.

The plants were so impressive. Gazing up, whistling Britney, I practically wanted to hug them, just like I almost ran away with my friends and joined a band at a certain point in my history when anything seemed possible, though the animals in the story just ended up tricking some robbers out of their house, eating their food, and curling up on the rug on their hearth. And now where are the tambourines? What is there, exactly, for me to put *myself* into? But let me wrap up, so to speak, take us the rest of the way around the block, so to speak, this side of the fence, with a few words about the value of shiny things floating icily in the constant state of becoming lost to us. Some time ago I started keeping a log of things and money I wasted. Some effort to contain them. A sweater left on a bench in the city (someone pick it up and use it?). A ticket for disrupting street sweepers (I'm sorry). Pie I ate all of that was nowhere even close to delicious.

THISTLES

Rosette stage early May, flower May to July, double dentate, toothed again, predicted soon to monopolize a large extent of country to the extinction of other plants, as they have done in parts of the American prairies, in Canada and British Columbia, and as they did in Australia, until a stringent Act of Parliament was passed, about twenty years ago, imposing heavy penalties upon all who neglected to destroy Thistles on their land, every man being now compelled to root out, within fourteen days, any Thistle that may lift up its head, Government inspectors being specially appointed to carry out the enforcement of the law. www.botanical.com/botanical/mgmh/t/thistl11.html for your information, if you care about what is happening in the world with regard to whatever constitutes the indigenous one moment to the next mixing thornily with mankind, I *dare* you to try to pull me.

MIRAGE

Postapocalypse, we were all still racist and clamoring for scraps of gold. I was still lusting after the girl who looked most like a fashion model. Maybe there is something to be done about those feelings but I was not doing it very much, not anymore! I felt a little freed to just want what I wanted, wherever that came from. Like maybe it's not my job at this point to have a problem with getting off on something when that's how I feel about it. No one calls anything natural anymore, not after what we did. Finally! *Natural* means something like dead.

But who am I kidding? As soon as the dust settled—and granted, there was a good deal of dust—even *that* lousy freedom wore off. Now, whenever she's charming, like the way she holds up that coconut in the bald light as if there's a decision left to be made, I try hard, in order to justify my lust, to imagine her as not nearly so pretty—to imagine her as someone like me. Would I be charmed then? Someone like me, considering the last remnant of something. How hot is that?

But as long as there is anything left there's a decision to be made. For instance, I have put out of my mind the bodies of the dead, just as in the past I put out of my mind the bodies of the destitute. I have put out of my mind what we did with all the bodies. Oh my body, my body image, your body, your body, my image of your body.

COMING TO LIFE

When the Circuit City really did go under in a pile of full-priced cables everyone was yelling about on the internet, it was like what happened to the banks was happening for real, instead of getting a letter in the mail about where your account was and sitting in your stupid kitchen trying to picture an account. When Ely went on over to check out Circuit City directly from being laid off, he hadn't even been there since prom 1988 but he wanted to see if everyone was acting insane or buying something for the first time since when they got a stereo put into their El Camino with savings from their job at the PD Quix, which was what Ely did right before prom. I didn't get a stereo. I didn't have a car until after Mom lost her eyesight and then my dad died and I inherited his so I could drive her around. Ely went there as if to meet an old friend he'd drifted apart from through the years. I'm thinking of a friend of mine whose brother went schizophrenic when we were in school and I didn't get why we weren't connecting anymore, and then a few years later when my brother went schizophrenic it was "holy shit now I get it" and we were friends again. But this example seems funnier to me because one of the friends is an enormous red electronics store near a mall that everyone's hated since 1995. Everyone I know always hated it, including those of us who went mad. But Ely felt the cord of kinship. On the way—he drove imagining his car bursting with loot—he was thinking about the end of the movie of *Fight Club*, the skyline of corporate headquarters collapsing. The first time he saw the movie, in the multiplex, it felt so shocking, impressive, exhilarating, like the multiplex might collapse around them, everyone in it together. The next time he saw the movie was on video, showing it to a girl he was dating, on his couch at home, which suddenly seemed so crappy the second it was clear to him that she was not impressed with the movie, yeah whatever, corporations suck, crappy couch forever sinking in crappy apartment. But now, approaching the Circuit City, speeding within a tangle of highways called The Maze, city skyline across the water, he was feeling epic, high on something like the not-yet-reality of losing his job, like the movie was coming to life. He engaged in a little fantasy of bumping into that girl and having it come up, the prophetic movie ending from that lousy date—she'd have to be the one to bring it up, though—and she'd say something like, "You know, Ely, now I get why you were into that movie—it's so interesting when an image falls in and out of relevance through time like that, it really makes the nature of reality come alive," and he'd say something about yeah and sources of power, plug, plugging, plug you.

When he got to the store, there was one tight clump of cars in the humongous parking lot as close as possible to the doors and he found a space in the clump to pull into. He was not in the long-gone El Camino, he was in a Pontiac Bonneville that had been a gift from his in-laws before his divorce. He'd been treating it badly since the split and the whole thing was pilled and damp. He got out and leaned against it, taking in the view. The Circuit City was not 100 percent red like the one from his youth, it was camel with red markings. He was unsure whether this classed it up or down. He tried to remember the inside of the Circuit City he had pictured revisiting, moody and dark-lit, shopping for his car stereo in the best shape of his life, a guy buying a stereo for his car, irreproachable as coming of age throughout history, in this place that looked a lot like nightclubs on soap operas, invisible walls and neon. He remembered walking down the path of linoleum between carpeted regions, enormous console systems to the east and household appliances to the west. He remembered a pudgy lady with the tightly curled hair of the time and a face lit like a radish who looked at him and then looked into the depths of a clothes-washing machine, exactly like a person looking into a toilet, wanting so badly to throw up and not quite able to do it. He remembered the money in his pocket for the stereo for the car. Then he felt it in his brain, a microscopic electronic switch spasm going: dated, dated her, dated movie, car, store, dated, and even though he could feel the hands of time pushing him from behind, he could not make himself go into that store with all that coded, inorganic, and somehow still expiring material, but then if he didn't go in he was trapped, just standing there in the parking lot with his severance.

But what do I know. Since my dad died no one here has had a job, no one here has health insurance. I'm in the kitchen with my mother who is now going deaf. My brother keeps us in sight but just out of reach, too afraid to relax in the house and too afraid to leave it, and I can see his point because this place is falling the fuck apart.

A MORE PRACTICAL APPROACH

He didn't focus on the apocalypse because he couldn't do anything about it, and when he looked around, there still appeared to be plenty of life happening. He hung out with some woodsy handyman types who he thought would take him along if it came to that. As a kid, when things got tough, he'd mostly tried to teach his turtle how to read. He took scientific notes about his dog. He did enjoy seeing the giraffe being helicoptered over the city in a movie trailer. He liked mutants, hybrid people-animal-robots. He found himself interested in *origins* and not so much the other end of things beyond reach. It never crossed his mind until other people brought it up, which they did increasingly. Like they thought all their handyman skills would finally be appreciated. Meanwhile, he concentrated on saving some farm animals. He had some dogs to love in the now. Other people, they might have a boat, maybe some flares, some food and water, your basic earthquake preparedness, hand-crank radio, maybe some kind of a shelter. *Hopefully*, he thought, *I'll have enough money that I can just take a spaceship.*

JOURNALIST

This is a true story about a journalist and I don't care. A long time ago I was assisting a famous humanitarian-type professor in a course about literary and documentary ethics, and this guy Adam was enrolled. He wasn't in my discussion group—there were like eight groups and like two hundred people there to listen to the lectures—but somehow Adam decided he liked me of all people and started approaching me outside the beautifully repurposed soda factory where the class met. He was handsome, I knew, but for some reason it didn't matter to me, even though he was my age and had completed a degree at a fancy university I had once wanted to go to. I'd wanted to go to that university the same way you imagine you want to be a famous actress when what you mean is that you want to feel important.

So we chatted a few times I found pretty boring and then he asked if I would like to, I don't remember, something, so I told him no but I was walking home and if he wanted he could walk with me and hang out in the yard while I was gardening. It's worth mentioning here that I was one of the only white people living in a neighborhood with a lot of black and Mexican people, and I was one of the only people in the neighborhood who had anything to do with the university. I have been told, by people in my neighborhood, that I am very, very white. Adam, too, was white, white, white. So Adam took me up on my idea, walked along home with me, and he was cool with my dog, and it turned out he knew a lot more than I did about plants. He'd watch me and say this or that while I was poking around, and a pattern emerged. After class, he'd come up to me, I'd say, Well, I'm doing this or that, usually moving things around in my garden or taking the dog to the woods, come along if you want, and he started teaching me about plants we passed in the woods, wild white ginger, rattlesnake orchids. He brought me clippings from his place which he was having to sell because of the divorce he was going through, and he was saddest of all to lose all his plants. One afternoon he kissed me in the hallway near the bathroom. I was really angry about that, but then I started wondering what my problem was. He showed me a picture of his parents in a *Life* magazine spread from the '60s. He said they were friends with the Kennedys. He was always asking me if I thought he could be a good writer and I said I thought he could be a good journalist. He kept asking me and I kept saying the same thing in different ways. So after he kissed me and I was so mad about it, part of me started wanting him to kiss me again, maybe because of the handsome part, maybe because of the university part, maybe because of the Kennedys, or maybe the knowledge of plants, and at that point the whole dynamic shifted because he was so fucked up about his divorce and I was just so fucked up in general.

Let's see where this is going.

Shots rang out in the neighborhood one day while I was gardening in my yard with my dog watching, and my dog was killed. It was really crazy, caught on video, a total media event, and after I made a call across the country to this one person I used to be in love with, I called Adam. He's the one who lifted my dog into my truck and drove us to the woods, and he's the one who directed the bush-hog in the night to dig a hole and shine its headlamps while we moved the body, and he helped me cover the plot with rocks. The rocks were to keep it from getting dug up. Then I didn't hear from him, and then he told me, in our last telephone conversation, that he just couldn't take my level of pain, a phrase that stood out to me. But now he's a journalist. He has a nice place in the city and he flies all over the world and does stories about things like little brown girls being sold into prostitution. He's one of those journalists who presents every story without any ambiguity at all, who finds stories to tell in which there is no way to locate more than one way to feel about anything.

SIGNS

I drive by a motel when I need anything from the other side of town. Town's built like an hourglass, and there's a big lit sun shining from the motel sign, there at the waist. They put all the houses down here and all the stuff up there, so if I'm going to get anything I have to go by it. That's a pun.

And you wouldn't believe the congestion—no one in charge.

In the motel, pets are okay. There's a parking lot around the motel, and a rising hill of grass around that, like the bank of a moat. Wait until it really starts raining!

An hourglass. Figures. Because of time, running out, running errands, crappy town.

So I drive by, and this time it's day, with the sun over the sun. I see a woman's head doing a swivel, like behind the bank she's riding in a bumper car in a parking space. There's a dog on a leash; I can't see the dog, but I know it's there behind the land. This is suspicious, or prophetic, seeing someone's head but not whatever makes it do the things it does. The left hand doesn't know the right, brain squeezed out or removed like the ribs of Victorian ladies.

Then at night... I'm making my smoke run, my gin run... I tell you... the sun at night. It's not right. It's a symptom. It cancels everything out. But if I want anything in this place, it's down that one road. One rich farmer stuck a store in his field long ago and the town formed in relation to it.

Night, day. I think about getting by. It's hard to tell if I get any sleep. I feel pressure to do one thing or another. I don't know what to do. Sometimes I look up and say "Give me a sign!" but of course I'm kidding. I'll tell you the one for the Golden Nozzle Carwash: a giant showerhead raining gold on the silhouette of a sedan. You know what the sedan stands for. It stands for you and me. These are the signs in this town. Only a matter of time before something blows.

MINIONS

The minions lined their sneakers along the wall and then became two lines themselves, like teams at the end of a game, and each by each held hands and touched foreheads. They were past words. They'd been hollering and leafleting for months. They'd been psyching themselves up and out for years. They lay in their cots like orphans. Hands to hearts, eyes to the black air, the rafters of the bunker invisible in the dark, a sky without stars, everything celestial sprinkling the insides of their domed minds. They waited for the world to disintegrate. It would disintegrate before next light and they waited for a red and gold explosion to light the universe in one final burst. They listened to night tick through the wooden walls. It could be now, or now, or now. Someone held back a sneeze and then sneezed. They'd abandoned their timepieces in the river that evening at dusk, but at two a.m. a boy named Jonathan got up from his cot, cracked open the door, put his penis out, and peed. Then he went back to his cot. One woman, a secret doubter, had taken a bottle of pills before she lay down to wait and died with the click the boy made closing the door.

By morning there have been three more suicides and two of the leaders have disappeared into the woods. One leader is weeping under a tree, fallen leaves in his fists. One leader is running, running, running, hoping he will die mid-step, trying to feel the moment within each step when he is sure both feet are off the ground because he feels that if he can prolong that beat he will be flying, he will be without his body finally, he will be light, light air, light light. In the hut one minion has punched another in the chest. One is cross-legged on her cot, watching. She's vacant or else she's fuming. Three have closed themselves in the kitchen and begun to screw. Two are quietly packing their knapsacks, stuffing them as full as they can with any useful items the group had forgotten or not bothered to purge: a woolen lap blanket, a can-opener, a tin of olives, a box of matches, a comb, a tube of lip balm. By two o'clock in the afternoon the bunker is empty except for a few dead bodies and one man, badly beaten, who is clinging to his cot like it's a raft, gasping for breath and calling "Help! Help!"

MIRROR

Two days since the apocalypse and freckles rise in the skin around my mouth. I am very close to my face, looking. Green funnels of what were pastures whirl and spit in the background. The last bits of cities are like comets and pass behind my head as if I am shooting myself repeatedly, as if I shoot myself and the fireballs go in one ear and out the other. It's riveting. It's hypnotic. My face contains more colors than are left in the universe. I watched Miranda's teeth panic and run away. I watched Amber buckle. Now, in the mirror, there is no comparison. It's me, and everything, and that's all.

LUCKY

People were walking around in the street, everywhere, in their clothes, with their personalities like so many fish. People looking sharp as weapons in holsters—I'm talking potential for protection or striking out in equal but opposite directions. Minds in their bones, bones in their minds. Bones in the future and bones in the past, bones in clothes, with premonitions and shadows, fore and aft. Mid-morning, big engine sun banging

on cement and metal, and all the littler engines in the streets and buildings, in the cars and bodies. A blond girl squinted out the giant window
of the 7-Eleven, luckiest store in the world. She'd been connecting the
dots with her car, one lucky star to the next, across the bright city. She
wore a down coat. A girl rollerbladed by the window in a bikini, a bright
pink headband with plastic feathery fluff on it that made her feel the fur
lining of the hood of the girl on the other side. Three round and haloed
heads, counting the sun. The girl in the bikini rollerbladed back, did a
spin in front of the window and then leaned on a parked car, sucking on
a soda, contemplating the girl in the parka in the air-conditioned store.
She felt the condensation on her big cup. She felt her hip on a headlight.
Luck, or whatever luck is code for, is cold, unbalanced, and connected.

    Sad girl in her mania. Sunny girl with her pop. Looking through
glass as if it's a mirror. All these people. How did they do it? Well, many
did not.

IV.
THESE FINAL
APOCALYPSES

expansion, disintegration, ellipses

BATHING

One thing about after the apocalypse is you can't get dirt on you—I mean you can, but you better not—it stings and itches like crazy, and I don't know about you but I can't get anything accomplished if I don't feel clean. Plus water's a problem, even after everything. And sand—you know I read in a book when I was a kid about how to wash by scrubbing with sand—but now that's even worse—what would you expect, it's just another kind of dirt. Everything makes for one rash or another, some with welts, some with, well, stinking welts, or welts that take over your whole body, or welts that blend in with other people's welts, or the welts on the animals and trees, or the welts on the dirt and on the water. The whole point of the apocalypse was to feel clean. What a load.

BARBARIANS

It was exciting about the economy because the economy deserved it. I was angry when they kept propping it back up, but I was scared when I lost my job altogether and found it nearly impossible to think. Soon enough I couldn't find anything to eat. Then a guy I met went nuts, raped me and took my dog. He kept saying it was a matter of domestic policy, that was the vocabulary of his delusion. I kept thinking maybe it could all be for the better in the long run. I'm practical at heart. I got some guns and shot a few people I always knew were assholes, as long as the justice system was the last thing on our minds. That did something for society and me both. I shot a police. Then I found a bourgeoisie and shot him with another bullet I had and then pretended to be giving him some beans, and then I took the sharp edge of the can and cut his wrist with it for symbolic impact, like "you did this to yourself," while his stomach was all bleeding from the bullet. Then Olivia spotted me. I'd been travelling with her and this smudgy kitten she kept in her coat pocket, and she was so pissed when she saw what I'd done that she took her kitten out and let it scratch at my eyes. She was like, *You have lost all sense of perspective, that guy probably had a lot to contribute now that you fucked him up.* I was just crying because of everything, physical and mental at the same time. At first I thought the kitten would really scratch my eyes out, but then it just patted me with its claws retracted. I felt the pats of little kitten feet and felt I was not in it alone. But I don't know how long you can keep a kitten in this scenario.

IDEA

There should be a film starring people and a giant piece of paper that walks around with them, goes on picnics and everything. It definitely has text on it but you can never read it even though it's larger than life. It's the way the light hits that makes it so you can't read it. That's the best part. It's a sunny and tragic film.

SUPERPOWERS

No one saw her jump from the city's tallest luxury rental apartment building. Later that day a guest at a nearby hotel reported a body on the roof of a parking structure making a shape like frightened cartoon animals from her childhood. The guest and her partner in business and love, homeowners, car-leasers, personally know three additional people who killed themselves in or on parking structures (one a thing called a "carport") this year. There's yet another documentary going around about the guardrail-for-the-bridge debate. Clearly someone whose friend jumped is trying to be objective but freaking out behind the camera every single second. It's amazing how transparent a camera can be in a situation like that. The partners wonder by what superpower they are operating when they can see through the movie like that. They are driving around, looking for a parking spot for the thing they're doing after the movie, moving their perspective in and out so the world looks like the world, then like the world is just something playing in their windshield, and back again. They are always near a parking structure when they need one, but prefer to circle the city looking for a spot on the street. It's not the money; they have money. From above, they are drawing a sacred circle of protection around the parking structure as they circle for parking, but they don't tell each other, and they're not going inside the circle anyway. Don't they say that when people who jump off a bridge survive, they always say they wanted to live right after they jumped and were sure they were going to die?

FREEZE BOX (MAMA'S GOT A)

Now, in the near future, we'd already perfected the cryogenic freeze-box for some time. We used it for everything, for animal and vegetable, but best was we could crawl in there for grieving. Let the psychotic teen shoot our mother, let the caped man rape us. We crawled into our machine to work through it all in distant dreams. Over time the teen used her own cryogenic box to wait through the delusions, and over time the caped man slept his rage away. Those of us awake on earth walked peacefully, and when we couldn't walk we slept until we awoke to the clean air of past sadness. Freeze-boxes lined the hills and followed us like wagons but still came the end of the world. We saw it coming, and toward us it crept, over time, a horizon. We kept our cryogenic chambers near. We were getting so sad, watching it approach like soldiers. We gazed across our freeze-boxes, into the eyes of one another, waiting for the right moment. We didn't want to leave, because finally it was all so beautiful.

IDEA OF CHINA

This apocalypse takes place in Her Idea of India, I mean China, whoever's coming up faster. Last week a thousand more consciousnesses slipped south, just across the border. I am so ambitious. It's one of the things she used to love about me. Used to be when someone said South of the Border I knew they meant something dirty. I'd think, could I go there? *I've come a long way*, I want to say to her. But she's all the way across the room, looking out the window again. I line my sight up with the back of her head and it's the back of her head.

THE LONELY SHARD

She took her laptop into bed to look at baby animals, so that the pattern was hard world, soft bed, hard computer, soft baby animals. What's inside after that was hard to tell because the telescoping stopped. She looked at baby polar bears first because that's what got it started was feeling herself floating away from the melting-iceberg mainland on her lonely shard. She moved on to puppies, a particular breed she'd had as a child that her parents had gotten rid of when they moved, the dog floating deeper into her past with every moment she remained alive. Her carpet was endless, but the animals were all so good and wronged that she started feeling better. But just as she started feeling better a sick feeling seeped in to cover the inside of her stomach like fur. *Just keep looking at them*, she told herself. *It's good for you no matter why*. What would her male counterpart be doing? Looking at trucks? What would her destitute counterpart be doing? Counting stars? What would her animal counterpart be doing? Breathing, breathing, breathing.

CROWD

I have come to an aquarium. Here is a plexiglass column of water and silver fish. Each fish is like two fingers from my hand. The silver fish swim clockwise, they swim in a mass, the way little fish swim, in a cloud given form by the columnular tank. I can see this in the home of a bazillionaire among white sofas and a mishmash of Italian art. The bazillionaire likes how many fish there are in there, how they move like a machine, especially because of his appreciation for large amounts in small places. He can see that they are the axis of the planet, that they are turning the planet from their tank. The fish keep a constant speed that means the fish on the outside swim more slowly than the fish at the center. It's that mathematical. Occasionally a fish will turn backward and push against the silver current for a stroke or two and then flip back. It will make a rush from inside to outside or back again. Occasionally a fish will unhinge its jaw for a beat, as if to let the quiet water they are all rushing through wash its insides out. Together the fish beat a rhythm of moving forward, a counter-rhythm of a series of singing movements across the tank, and a third rhythm of the pulsing of jaws. There are only three rhythms visible, and still they are incomprehensible. The fish seem delicate and hollow. Their silver skin is bright and young but their faces and bones make them ancient. This is why I feel so sad: all the rest of the aquarium is dark. I wanted the world simpler because I wanted to take it in, and now that almost all of it is gone, it is still too much; it's so much that soon I close my eyes, as if I can join everything else that has gone dark, but then it's even worse because what happens when you close your eyes is that everything is possible again.

GRAPH

The difficulty of overcoming the hurdles left some straggling at the edges of the earth, and some leaping over them like spurts of oil from a deep pot of humanity. They'd reached a point and turned suicides. The earth was crowded with suicides, but those who were not offing themselves were mad with self-preservation. Crowds gathered into a crowd, forming a heap in the middle, the crowd climbing itself, rising into a mountain of people refusing to die. From the distance you could see one or another fall as from towers. But they were falling from each other. We have a graph of it.

CONVENTIONAL/WISDOM

A quickly absorbed protective lotion pampers the body and keeps it feeling perfectly comfortable. When you are in the throes of madness, if you are a boy, you may try to kill people, and if you are a girl, you may try to kill yourself. According to renowned experts, apocalypses, utopias, and the persistence of capitalism are all due to a cultural failure of imagination.

PREDATOR

Boats are in trees. Photocopy machines are on the beach. The rack-line is made of bodies making a pattern like high-quality jacquard. A hyena sniffs along. There's a bird that sees it coming. It's standing on the sand flapping, from the look of it, madly. I don't see what's keeping it from taking off. From where I've landed on the tip of a pile of rubble, I'm trying to tell if the ways that birds express themselves has changed. Maybe nothing terrible is impending and the hyena is approaching for a new reason. I am scanning myself for the mechanisms of anticipation. There are no words for what I discover. I use my new eyes to scan the periphery. I take note of and apprehend a series of impossible and/or unrecognizable elements in this landscape. I note what predates what, as if we are following each other around.

BINARY

He went directly to the wilderness with his big knife and Gore-Tex. He was no longer against hunting because when you're primal it's just Monday morning. His hunting companion was the guy from the other side of the world who pushed the button, but now they got on fine. There were two girls they were raising into wives back in the clearing at the hut with the technology. Sometimes the men butted heads in the clearing, but out here they were of one mind. He was from Atlanta and the other guy was from someplace Arabic, and they did not have any language in common. *It's like living on a golf ball*, thought the Atlanta guy. *It's like living on an orange*, thought the Arab guy in fucked-up imaginary translation. Because the Earth had been wiped clean of landmarks and geographic features, they had no idea where they were or what it had been before. None of the animals looked like animals from places. They all looked and sounded like radioactive animals with multiple limbs and eyes, most of them giant and amphibious, and they attacked not with teeth and claws but with the poisons they spat from their fingers and that oozed when touched. They attacked with smells, with gases. None of them would make a decent pet, and neither of the guys was even thinking about domestication. They'd both been city kids, and they just wanted to feed the girls. In one episode their first fight was going to be who got which, like in buddy movies; in another episode they'd share, in another episode everyone would be gay and work out reproduction as a practical matter, and in another episode it was a combination. But for now the two men were hunting amphibians and the binary was like clean air, clean water, like invisibility, and they dreamed of the x axis and the y axis finding each other's centers in space, magical, pure, and absolute.

VENN DIAGRAM

Her fear in the night was that her success made her like so many successful people she disdained, but she made a good case that she was exceptional. She thought people were only seeing the parts of her that were like other successful people, but the parts left over from that were actually the good parts. The parts left over for the successful people she knew were the bad parts. That lemon in the middle, the shady part of the Venn diagram—what was that? That was success. After the apocalypse she was dead anyway, but her work remained. Survivors crowded around it. Everything was black, but it glowed white. They discarded the part that had been the lemon because one thing's for sure: everything had changed. They looked at what was left, and some of them wondered if this could be the new now. They remembered the stuff they'd always secretly loved or hated. One of them, a man, picked it up by the edge, lifted one crescent moon of it from the other, hooked it to his belt loop. *This could be my ticket*, he thought. Idiot.

ONE THING

Those two are as alike as eggs, but one small, one big. Sisters who could share clothes except for that one thing. "Are you sisters?" people are always saying. Both are physicists, except one's applied and one's theoretical. One is not mature—she throws fits, won't button up, can't fly right, and one will put an arm around her and say "sugar," like clockwork, or a fool in the wind, because while one's sweet one's kind of a jerk.

They're going through their things because they want a baby and who should have it?

One has brothers. Attributes: Buck's handsome, Tom's kind, Sam's never sick. Like a logger, like a turnip, as an ox. One has friends: George works in Africa, Barton's a playboy, Heinrich doesn't come out of his shed. If they're secretly eying a sperm bank they won't admit it. They don't like the odds. They call it a crapshoot. They'd rather play god if possible. Again: scientists.

"You, you, you," they say into each other's faces when they're happy and when they're mad.

People are always saying, "What if you end up with two? Or four? Or more!"

You only go into physics if you think you can figure it out.

One's younger, one's older, but not much.

One has genes that make her small and wary of her body.

One has Latina Birthing Hips and can swim a mile.

One is afraid of what the baby will say about her mother.

One is rough and tumbles like a dog.

One has a way with teens and one is a whiz in the kitchen (especially baking).

One has a therapist and one has an active ex. You know what? They can't figure it out.

They decide on an experiment: they'll both go for it and let fate duke it out with the stars. Then they'll know... something. They'll know one thing.

They take the drugs and baste away. They take their temperatures behind closed bathroom doors. They horde genius sperm culled from private deals in midnight hospital parking lots, sign contracts composed by lawyers they did coke with in school. They begin to see separate doctors and their calendars grow increasingly encoded. They spend their money down and pace their carpeted apartment.

Now, when they lie on their sides they eye each other's bellies as if. When they cuddle all they think of is being round.

One is two steps ahead. One is throwing the match.

People are always thinking, *What are you thinking?*

But something is changing as they recede into themselves. They are turning their backs to us as to each other. They are walking into the future, into a great pink egg light.

IDEODROME

Mudslides in Pakistan were claiming masses. Celebrities flocked to toxic New Orleans. Zebras contracted anthrax in Africa. Tsunamis elicited tales of terror. Before him, the ideodrome rose from Earth, glowing like a lampshade, underdeveloped ideas swimming electrically beneath the opalescent surface. He remembered the time he arrived home drunk and noticed, just as the suspended tennis ball in the garage touched the roof of his car and stopped him from running the car through the back wall, that he'd been driving with a dead motorcyclist shot through his windshield. He thought of an idea piercing the surface of the ideodrome and making its way along the molecules of the air, sliding into his mouth and filling it with the breath of knowledge. He looked up and a raindrop hit his forehead. Like a splash, his awareness expanded and he could see he was part of a crowd of people surrounding the ideodrome, that the people were like the particles that made up the ring of Saturn back when it seemed to have just the one ring, that the people looked computer-generated until another drop of rain hit him on the tiny bald spot on his crown where all his hair started, and suddenly he could smell how bad everyone smelled and see how everyone was wearing rags or Nike shirts from the '90s, how they had incense stuck in their hair and scars on their faces and a lot of warped limbs. Then the ring was the ring of poverty around a great city, and the great city was of one mind that was not his own. Then he approached the ideodrome with his hand out. But an emaciated claw sprang from the crowd and yanked him back by his asshole elbow.

RATE THIS APOCALYPSE

He led her to a long white table, so clean, so cold, so bare, but for the apocalypses laid out in grid formation, uncountable, bouncing like icons waiting for updating, little puff of smoke in the grid, little lightning bolt, little funnel cloud, tiny tsunami, dancing flame, microscopic viruses magnified to match the rest, matchstick aliens, monsters like the figures on coins, anything you ever wanted. He said choose. The large print said to rate them but the small print said, in bed. She thought about choosing one of each, but he said it was one for each of us on Earth. He said each one was a little different, if only by nurture. He said she could rank based on her individual criteria. He said overall satisfaction, with a wink. She looked at him funny, and he laughed in cartoon under his dated mustache. She said skeptically that she would never consent to sleep with him, not in a million years. He said he'd fill out the form for her if she couldn't handle it. He said the world was her oyster, blowing in the wind, if she'd only open her mind. She let several of the apocalypses run up her sleeve, down her pants, and enter her body while he wasn't looking. She let them look out of her eyes. She crept up behind him while he was looking under the table for the missing animations, used an apocalypse on his pants so they collapsed around his ankles where they belonged, and made a run for it.

FERTILE CRESCENT

Starting over ours was the valley that became the next fertile crescent. This was in my own lifetime. The people in the projects I live next to rioted and burned the city, but my house and Sam's were in a special bubble, so we're unscathed to the bitter end.

I'm cultivating dark earth, and with a quick pan you can see, furrow after furrow, how much I've already accomplished. Still, this vague unease under it that I participated in or even started the riots with a rock, or a can, or a rumor. Then it's as if I led the rioters away from my house, but I can't remember. There's my house at the edge of the furrows.

Even with my hoe and my spade I keep thinking about Allende, just as an example, shooting himself in a room that keeps looking like the oval office. He's shooting himself just as the soldiers peep their heads in the windows after climbing a rose trellis outside. He's shooting himself because he tried something and now this.

Despite everything, after the apocalypse there are hardly any suicides, no matter what we've done or failed to do. I suppose our minds assure us we can handle it. I mean God only gives you... I mean God only lets you do what you can live with after the apocalypse. After the apocalypse, we're just living with ourselves.

FUNERAL

When everyone's favorite leader died, everyone lined up to see him. They filled the flowery valley and filed by for weeks. It's understandable that they wanted to see him, still and eternal, in his coffin. But after days and nights, when the line showed no sign of ending, some of the guards suspected that some people were getting back in line and filing by again.

They started stamping people's hands and gave that some time to work, but maybe people rubbed the ink off, and word had not come down about how to decide where to put an end to it, the line. This was a *very great leader*. What if you were the last one to file by or the first one refused? Could you be the one to make that happen, even with the official hat? It would be like holding one person above everyone else, plus everyone's love of the leader was equal; that's what made him so great. It's important, in a ceremony like this, to be anonymous so that you can represent everyone who can't make it (though in this case it was hard to picture, with all the people lining up, that anyone might not have made it). They felt that if they drew the line it'd be so arbitrary, and the man still made people feel that even if the world was arbitrary, he'd forge a path for them through it. Maybe the people felt this too, that if there was an end of the line they'd throw the meaning of the man off balance, because people kept getting on line. Guards were getting on line in their hats. They loved the man, too, like everyone. You could look and look and not be able to tell how the line went; it coiled for a while but then it was just a buzzing wad of people that only dissipated, presumably, in the mountains, wherever the flowers petered out. But time was marching on. Once the leader started to decay they thought maybe that would end it, but perfume vendors appeared like flies and at first people used their pocket change for perfume, but soon it became a matter of bravado to see him, to endure or wallow in the loosed particles of him that created the smell. People breathed him. They watched each other breathe him so that they could breathe him together, and they felt he lived again as part of them. Ending it would be like performing an execution.

Then they thought: *Wait a cotton-pickin' minute. He is dead. This is out of control.* They formed a new line so that they could approach the old line. They drew their guns. Now it was us and them.

JAGUAR (NOT THE CAR)

I had just seen the jungle for the first time in my rotten life, centuries-old ferns everywhere, so moving. When you are in the jungle you have to remember the herds of pigs: *hundreds*, possibly *thousands*, will chase a jaguar up a tree and piss on the tree through the night until the ammonia makes the cat pass out and fall from the tree, and they eat him in a pile of hooves and spots.

As he is disintegrating, these are my old pal Tony's last words of advice to me from his days in Nicaragua: tie your ass to the tree. Then, as we used to say, he was gone.

When the dust cleared there I was, and on the horizon, there's the tree, as if he knew all along. I hadn't seen him since we were young turks. We were letting bygones be gone but I could see certain pains in his eyes. Some left over from when I left. When the rumbling started we were pretty drunk and we loved the band. Now I eye the tree across the border, in Nicaragua, his past, my future. I'm so wiped out from the whole experience, I don't know what to do in this bald new vista. I wonder if I really have to head out to it, to that one tree I can see, just because it's still there. Then I hear rumbling. Possibly aftershock. I hear the roar of what could be thousands.

BODY

After graduation, their daughter's madness burst from her head full-grown. By the time she was pronounced dead of medications, she was bloated with fluids and bubble-wrapped in the watery light of the ICU, with tubes and the green hum of numbers reflecting on the walls. Blisters like jellyfish rose on her knuckles from being pressed to the carpet under her body weight. No one is blaming the people lined up for organs. The mother and the father stood over her in every way you can think of. The father put ointment on her eyes and closed the lids. Next is a line about the father that I can't write. Next is a line about the mother. Next is a line about there and not there. Then on the morning of the fourth day, their daughter woke up. She made noise through her tube. She said, "I drowned?" She pointed out some hallucinations. When she saw her fingers down the blanket, she guessed carrots. The carrots were down at the edge of her body, over near her parents as part of the skyline, pointing at any number of endings.

VACATION

The only cars left are tour vans and taxis. The visitors are from the country that provided the military. It's upstairs-downstairs but continents. The last thing we remember is the sheen of all possible vacations. I was in the gift shop, choosing between a colorful calendar (*Girls of the Apocalypse*) and a colorful coffee-table book (*Voices from the Apocalypse*). The guides, no matter who they're working for, share a special language of their own. Empty mountains echoed with their calls.

ISLANDS

We were drifting closer and closer to those islands in the shapes of continents off the coast of Dubai where you could buy Africa or someplace and put your house on it, dock a yacht. From above, the shape of our continent of plastic bags and bottles was the shape of one really desolate guy. He used to be the size of Manhattan, but between that and the whole USA we'd lost perspective.

MINDLESS

When the globe that meant the world to me fell from my hands and burst, I left the room, and when my love, or whatever I meant by her, came into the room accidentally, she saw that the air conditioning was like those videos of rock bands in vacant fields, deserts, with their hats, rocky outcroppings of emotion, no one listening out there but the fans.

AFTER

What was left? An enormous collection of transparencies. We couldn't be more minimal. That plastic cup, including the ice. Your lenses. A stack of tracing paper, also tracing paper in the wind, and wind. Think of the bottles and bottles of water. Including thinking. A matter of clear glass vs. clear plastic, vs. gin vs. vodka vs. tap vs. Voss. A room with two doors in shotgun fashion. I'll stand in this one. I couldn't care less. It looks like static coming down hand over fist. Now, if you stood in that opening you'd ruin it. You can't even come in because of the enormous collection wobbling invisibly.

WHAT IT WAS LIKE WAS

Stars fell in unison, and in a mossy grove on the hill, the Apocalyptasaurus was having the last sex on earth. I headed to the mobile unit. I hadn't brought any animals because that's how shortsighted I am. *Something will provide*, I seemed to be thinking, but who knows anymore, I haven't had to think in so long I don't even know when I'm doing it or not. I drifted away. Unpeopling, repeopling, all in the past with the automatic sprinklers, and soon the cries of leftover apocalypses were all that remained. Some of the things we knew were true. I'd only wanted to keep the bells ringing.

"Eyes of Dogs" first appeared in *Conjunctions* online and is a version of Hans Christian Andersen's "The Tinderbox."

"Madmen" first appeared in *American Short Fiction*. The scenes that take place in the asylum "gallery" paraphrase or collage sections from *Seeing the Insane* by Sander Gilman (University of Nebraska Press, 1996). Occasional lines are paraphrased from the first chapters of Michel Foucault's *History of Madness*.

"Godzilla Versus the Smog Monster" (now much altered) first appeared in *Gargoyle*.

Some of the apocalypses first appeared, most in different form, along with additional apocalypses, in the following publications: *The Apocalypse Reader*, *Black Warrior Review*, *Caliban*, *Devil's Lake*, *Diagram*, *Eleven Eleven*, *Filter*, *Gulf Coast*, *Hobart*, *The Huffington Post*, *The Laurel Review*, *The Massachusetts Review*, *Quarter After Eight*, *Rampike*, *Sou'Wester*, *Swink*, *Tarpaulin Sky*, *Tin House* (flash fiction blog), *West Branch*, *Wigleaf*.

Thanks to the 2009 Radar Productions Akumal Lab Rats and so many others who shared their apocalypses and helped me wrestle with mine, including: Joe Atkins, Lisa Hanks Baxter, Kate Bernheimer, Suzanne Bost, Shannon Cain, Andrea Cohen, Nicole J. Georges, Emily Hochman, Howard Hochman, Pam Houston, Laurie Lewis, Ali Liebegott, Melissa Malouf, John Marx, Shelly Oria, Beth Pickens, Tim Ramick, Christine Schutt, Michael Snediker, Justin Taylor, Laura Egley Taylor, Michelle Tea, John Vincent, and Kevin Wilson.

Thanks especially to PJ Mark and Ethan Nosowsky.

ABOUT THE AUTHOR

Lucy Corin is the author of the short story collection *The Entire Predicament* and the novel *Everyday Psychokillers: A History for Girls*. She won the 2012 American Academy of Arts and Letters Rome Prize and was the recipient of a Creative Writing Fellowship from the National Endowment for the Arts. She lives in San Francisco and teaches at the University of California at Davis.

FINE, FINE, FINE, FINE, FINE
by DIANE WILLIAMS

"A taut collection of flash fictions that are often
beautiful but impenetrable, structured like little
riddles to unspool." —*The New York Times*

The very short stories of Diane Williams have been aptly called "folk tales
that hammer like a nail gun," and these forty new ones are sharper than
ever. They are unsettling, yes, frequently revelatory, and more often than
not downright funny.

Not a single moment here is what you might expect. While there is
immense pleasure to be found in Williams's spot-on observations about how
we behave in our highest and lowest moments, the heart of the drama beats
in the language of American short fiction's grand master, whose originality,
precision, and power bring the familiar into startling and enchanted relief.

store.mcsweeneys.net

ADIOS, COWBOY
by OLJA SAVIČEVIĆ

"A glorious new European voice has emerged."
—*The Guardian*

This American debut by a poet from Croatia's "lost generation" explores a beautiful Mediterranean town's darkest alleys: the bars where secrets can be bought, the rooms where bodies can be sold, the plains and streets and houses where blood is shed. By the end of the long summer, the lies, lust, feuds, and frustration will come to a violent and hallucinatory head.

store.mcsweeneys.net

MY DOCUMENTS
by ALEJANDRO ZAMBRA

"This dynamite collection of stories has it all—Chile and
Belgium, exile and homecomings, Pinochet and Simon and
Garfunkel—but what I love most about the tales is their
strangeness, their intelligence, and their splendid honesty."
—Junot Díaz, *The New Yorker*

My Documents is the latest work from Alejandro Zambra, the award-winning
Chilean writer whose first novel was heralded as the dawn of a new era in
Chilean literature, and described by Junot Díaz as "a total knockout." Now,
in his first short story collection, Zambra gives us eleven stories of liars and
ghosts, armed bandits and young lovers—brilliant portraits of life in Chile
before and after Pinochet. Zambra's remarkable vision and erudition is on
full display here; this book offers clear evidence of a sublimely talented
writer working at the height of his powers.

store.mcsweeneys.net

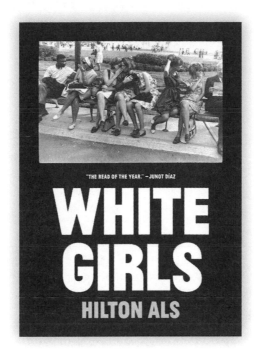